The only light in the room came from the fire....

"Look," Christiana said quietly to Dillon, "I know that my qualifications are less than stellar. But I'm a good person, and I'm genuinely fond of children. If you'd just give me a chance, you'd find that I'm ideal for the job."

Dillon looked at her for a long time before speaking. "All right. You have my okay. My daughter Katy is with my parents for the rest of the week. If she likes you when she gets back, the job is yours."

Christiana honestly didn't know if she was glad or not. She'd certainly gotten what she came for. "Thank you."

Dillon looked at her for a moment longer, then left.

Christiana stared into the fire. Everything was falling into place, just the way her parents had planned it. She was here, in this house . . . with her dead sister's mysterious husband.

Dear Reader,

Though it may be cold outside during the month of November, it's always warmed by the promise of the upcoming holiday season. What better time to curl up with a good book? What better time for Silhouette Romance?

And in November, we've got some wonderful books to take the chill off these cold winter months. Continuing our DIAMOND JUBILEE celebration is *Song of the Lorelei*, by Lucy Gordon. Escape to the romantic world of brooding Conrad von Feldstein. The haunting secret at von Feldstein Castle is revealed when beautiful Laurel Blake pays a visit . . . and love finally comes home. Don't miss this emotional, poignant tale!

The DIAMOND JUBILEE—Silhouette Romance's tenth anniversary celebration—is our way of saying thanks to you, our readers. To symbolize the timelessness of love, as well as the modern gift of the tenth anniversary, we're presenting readers with a DIAMOND JUBILEE Silhouette Romance each month, penned by one of your favorite Silhouette Romance authors. And rounding up the year, next month be sure to watch for *Only the Nanny Knows for Sure*, by Phyllis Halldorson.

And that's not all! There are six books a month from Silhouette Romance—stories by wonderful writers who, time and time again, bring home the magic of love. During our anniversary year, each book is special and written with romance in mind. This month, and in the future, work by such loved writers as Diana Palmer, Brittany Young and Annette Broadrick is sure to put a smile on your face.

During our tenth anniversary, the spirit of celebration is with us year-round. And that's all due to you, our readers. With the support you've given to us, you can look forward to many more years of heartwarming, poignant love stories.

I hope you'll enjoy this book and all of the stories to come. Come home to romance—Silhouette Romance—for always!

Sincerely,
Tara Hughes Gavin
Senior Editor

BRITTANY YOUNG

The House
by the Lake

Silhouette *Romance*

Published by Silhouette Books New York

America's Publisher of Contemporary Romance

SILHOUETTE BOOKS
300 E. 42nd St., New York, N.Y. 10017

ISBN: 0-373-08759-4

First Silhouette Books printing November 1990

Printed in the U.S.A.

Books by Brittany Young

Silhouette Romance

BRITTANY YOUNG

lives and writes in Racine, Wisconsin. She has traveled to most of the countries that serve as the settings for her Silhouette Romances and finds the research into the language, customs, history and literature of these countries among the most demanding and rewarding aspects of her writing.

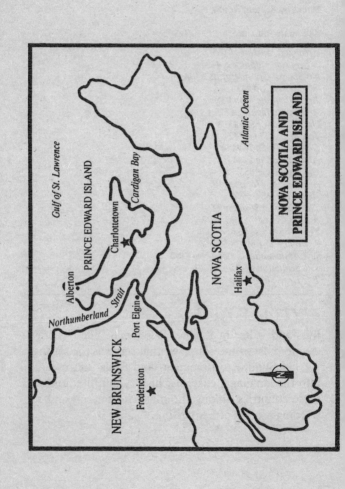

Gulf of St. Lawrence

PRINCE EDWARD ISLAND

Cardigan Bay

Charlottetown

Alberton

Northumberland *Strait*

Port Elgin

NEW BRUNSWICK

Fredericton

NOVA SCOTIA

Halifax

Atlantic Ocean

NOVA SCOTIA AND
PRINCE EDWARD ISLAND

N

Prologue

Christiana Jean Stevenson White sat curled up on the couch in the cozy den of her Chicago apartment reading a good book. Such a good book that when the telephone rang and she reached for the receiver on the table beside her, she kept on reading. "Hello," she said absently.

"Hi, C.J."

She looked up from her book and frowned at the sound of her sister's voice. "Paige! Where have you been? Mom and Dad have been trying to get in touch with you all week. Today they upgraded themselves from worried to frantic."

"I'm in New York, but that's not important. Wait until you hear my news!"

"What news?"

"I'm married."

Christiana sat up straight. "Married? Since when?"

"Just yesterday."

"Oh, Paige, how could you?"

Paige exhaled in exasperation. "I knew you wouldn't be happy for me. This is so typical. I call you with wonderful news and you say 'Oh, Paige, how could you?'"

"Did you, for one minute, stop to think about how this is going to hurt Mom and Dad? How could you get married without even telling them, much less inviting them?"

"I couldn't invite anyone. Dillon wanted everything kept completely private. I'll send them some flowers. They'll get over it. They always do. And you can run a little interference for me."

Sometimes Christiana felt as though she'd spent half of her life running interference for Paige. She closed her book and leaned against the back of the couch. Her silky dark hair spread out around her. "Are you happy?" she asked quietly.

"Ecstatically, unbelievably happy."

"Which one of your men friends is the lucky man?"

"Dillon Austin."

"Dillon Austin? *The* Dillon Austin who composes the music for The Vancouver Band?"

"One and the same."

"I'm impressed. I didn't even know you knew him."

"We famous models know everyone who's anyone. I think I mentioned him to Mom in one of my letters."

"How long have you been seeing him?"

"Just a few weeks. But I knew he was the one the first time I laid eyes on him. Oh, C.J., he's the most wonderful man I've ever met. He's everything I've ever wanted in a man but could never find until now. You'll see when you meet him."

Christiana was skeptical. She knew the kind of man her sister was usually attracted to. Beautiful on the outside, empty on the inside. She truly hoped this one was different. "And when will that be?"

"Probably not for quite a while. He's very busy just now. But if you turn on your television in about one minute, you'll get to see him being interviewed."

"What channel?"

"I'm not sure. I know it's one of the big three."

"All right. I'll watch."

"Give my love to Mom and Dad."

"I will. And, Paige? Congratulations. I want you to be happy, you know."

"I will be—now."

As soon as she'd hung up, Christiana reached for her remote control and turned on the television set, then started flipping channels until she found a talk show. The host was in the middle of asking a question, but that wasn't what interested Christiana anyway. She wanted to see Dillon.

The camera panned over the men seated on the stage. This, she knew, was The Vancouver Band. She had a vague recollection of what Dillon looked like. Neither he nor the rest of the band members sought publicity. They tended to let their remarkable music speak for them.

But as soon as she saw him, she knew which one he was. Her smoky blue eyes zeroed in on him.

The first thing she noticed was how attractive he was. He was dressed casually in a sport coat over faded jeans. His body was long and strong-looking, even seated. His black hair was long in back, curling slightly over his shirt collar. His face was handsome and lived in, with laugh lines next to his eyes and grooves in his cheeks even when he wasn't smiling—which he wasn't at the moment. He was, she guessed, about thirty-five. His eyes were warm and intelligent and when he spoke, as he was doing now, his voice was deep and quietly rich. She found herself wondering why he never sang, with a voice like that.

Christiana learned a lot about her new brother-in-law just by watching him. He was quiet and reflective, and at times very funny. He was relaxed and articulate and every bit as intelligent as his eyes had made him seem when she'd first looked at him.

But there was a reserve about him. Even the few times he smiled, there was something behind the smile she couldn't quite put her finger on. As a still photographer who was used to interpreting peoples' expressions, it intrigued her. Dillon intrigued her.

The host's question about his recent marriage caught her attention and with interest she watched Dillon's reaction. Instead of the look of a man who was pleased with the new turn his life had taken,

Dillon grew silent. She saw the muscle in his jaw move, yet nothing in his expression gave away his thoughts. "I'd prefer to keep my personal life private," he finally said.

The host backed off instantly and moved the questioning on to some charitable work the men were involved in as a group and as individuals.

Again, she listened and watched. When the program was over, Christiana turned off the television and sat unmoving on the couch, lost in her thoughts.

Dillon Austin hadn't been what she'd expected. Considering his fame and what he did for a living, he was remarkably sane. A definite improvement in Paige's usual taste in men.

But what had that lack of expression on Dillon's face meant when he'd been asked about his marriage?

Chapter One

Three years later...

Christiana stood by the small lake and gazed at the clear, calm water. It was beautiful here. Exquisitely beautiful. Not at all the kind of place where she'd expect a man like Dillon Austin to live.

After tucking her shoulder-length dark hair behind her ears, she raised her camera and focused the telephoto lens on a wooden dock that jutted perhaps fifteen feet into the water. A skiff with two oars and no motor undulated gently on the water. A long rope ran from the front of the skiff to a cleat at the edge of the dock. The shutter of Christiana's camera clicked and the film advance whirred.

She turned toward a charming white farmhouse set on a nearby hill. A long veranda went all the way around the house and a freshly painted white fence separated the yard from the rest of the farmland. The barn was set slightly lower on the hill and there were also some smaller sheds that probably housed equipment and tools.

So this was Lakecroft. She aimed the camera. Click. Whirrr.

Slinging the camera strap over her shoulder, Christiana put the tips of her fingers into the pockets of her faded jeans and started walking around the lake. Her feet shuffled through the bright yellow, orange and red leaves that were just beginning to fall from the trees. This was her first time on Prince Edward Island, and Christiana couldn't help but wonder if the entire island was as beautiful as this particular place.

The trees along the lake bank grew more numerous the farther she walked, until the lake, which had grown narrower and more shallow, seemed to become part of a forest. And then the forest became part of the lake where trees grew right out of the water. She'd never seen anything like it.

Wishing that there was more light, she adjusted the shutter speed to compensate, raised the camera to her eye, studied the scene through the viewfinder, and snapped a picture.

Letting the camera fall back on its strap, she stayed there for several minutes, just to gaze at her surroundings and listen. The silence was remarkable. Perhaps the air was too brisk to entice the frogs to sing. It was already four-thirty in the afternoon, so the birds were finished for the day and the nighttime insects hadn't taken over yet.

Suddenly an owl hooted.

Christiana turned her head in the direction she thought the sound had come from, but saw nothing. She had no idea what the proper name for this place was, but for her, from that moment, it became The Sanctuary. A place where a person could come whenever she needed to leave everything else behind and wanted only to find peace of mind and spirit. She hadn't felt this quiet inside since Paige had been killed.

Almost regretfully she continued her walk, moving slowly, gazing up at the sky through the bright leaves and watching the way the late-afternoon light filtered down through them. She could just imagine how glorious this place would be in the morning.

And then the trees began to thin until they were once again scattered along the lake bank. She crossed an old wooden footbridge that led about two hundred feet from one side of the lake to the other, and climbed over a slatted log fence that enclosed a cleared pasture.

A wiry middle-aged man carrying a walking stick was tugging on the lead cow to get her moving. As soon as the animal started walking with him, six other cows followed along behind, the big bells at their throats clanking in rhythm with the languid sway of their hips. The man spotted Christiana and politely inclined his head toward her. She smiled back, raised her camera and took another picture, then just watched until they disappeared over a low hill.

The crisp fall breeze blew a little harder, sending a chill through her. Christiana rubbed her arms through her heavy sweater, but she didn't really mind the cold. It was worth it just to smell the fresh, clean air.

As soon as she started walking again, she spotted a small woods in the middle of the pasture and walked toward it, anxious to see what wonders she'd find there. Two beautiful Irish setters, their coats silky and long, came racing out as she approached and began wagging their tails madly in anticipation of a good petting, bumping against her, but far too well mannered to jump.

"Hello, you beautiful babies," Christiana said as she knelt on the ground and dug her fingers into their silky fur, laughingly turning her head this way and that to avoid their affectionate tongues.

Then, just as quickly as they'd come, they took off across the field. "Was it something I said?" she yelled after them.

Getting to her feet, she brushed herself off and continued walking. She was perhaps within fifteen feet of entering the woods when a huge black horse suddenly crashed through the trees and galloped full tilt straight at her. She froze in fear, unable to even scream. The man on the horse saw her and pulled back hard on the reins just before the horse would have run her down. The powerful animal reared high in the air. One of its front hooves clipped a glancing blow on her shoulder and the side of her head, sending her reeling back and crashing to the ground. It took the man a few seconds to bring the horse under control, but as soon as he did, he leaped from its back and ran to Christiana.

"Oh, my God," he said as he knelt beside her. "Where the hell did you come from?"

Christiana tried to raise herself onto her elbows, still slightly stunned. "I was just taking some pictures," she managed to say.

He pressed her gently back to the ground. "Haven't you ever heard of private property?"

"I didn't think . . ."

"Obviously. Stop moving until I've had a chance to look you over."

Christiana tried to sit up again. "I'm fine."

"You aren't fine. You're bleeding. Now lie still."

As he leaned over her, Christiana found herself looking at the man she'd come here to see. Dillon Austin. There was no mistaking him. He looked just as he had on television nearly three years earlier.

He took off his jacket and draped it over her, then took off his shirt and used it to dab at the blood she could feel trickling down her face. As he leaned over her, Christiana found herself confronted with a choice of either closing her eyes or staring at his nicely muscled chest. Since when were rock musicians built like that?

"Ouch!" she suddenly yelped when he hit a tender spot.

"Sorry," the man apologized as he swung his eyes to her smoky blue ones. "It doesn't seem too serious. I don't think you're going to need any stitches but you should see a doctor anyway. Do you think you can sit up?"

"Yes."

He helped her into a sitting position. The jacket slid onto her lap. "How do you feel?" he asked, looking closely at her.

Her head was throbbing. "Fine."

"Fine?" he asked skeptically.

"All right," she conceded. "Let's say fine, but not as well as I did before your horse assaulted me."

The man lifted an expressive eyebrow. "Assaulted you?"

"What would you call it?"

"Trespassing."

A corner of Christiana's mouth lifted despite herself. "So I was. I guess I got what I deserved."

He looked at her in surprise. "Well, someone who can admit she's wrong. I think I like you already."

"Oh good. Now I can die a happy woman," she said dryly.

Two deep grooves etched themselves in his cheeks. "You hit back. I'll have to remember that. Take off your sweater."

She looked at him and blinked once. "I beg your pardon?"

"I want to look at your shoulder. In order for me to do that you'll have to take off your sweater."

She still hesitated.

"Lady, I assure you I'm not some maniacal mass murderer on the loose from the local asylum."

"I bet that's what all maniacal mass murderers tell their potential victims."

"Probably."

"I really don't think this is necessary," Christiana told him as she slid her good arm out of the sleeve, then gingerly worked on the other one.

The man grew impatient.

"I'm sorry, but I seem to be having a little trouble with this one—I can't lift my arm as high as I need to. Would you help me, please?"

He deftly managed to pull the sweater over her head and then peel the other sleeve from her arm. With surprisingly gentle hands, he unbuttoned her blouse and slid it from her injured shoulder. "The skin isn't broken," he said after a moment, his head close to hers, "but it's already starting to bruise. How high are you able to raise it?"

Christiana didn't hear a word he said. She was wrapped in her thoughts as she stared at the top of his head. If she could have run away at that moment, she would have. This wasn't right. She shouldn't have come.

"Are you still there?" he asked as he pulled back a little and looked at her.

Her eyes met his. "I beg your pardon?"

"I asked you how high you could raise your arm."

She managed to lift it to shoulder height.

"Can you lift it higher?"

"Of course I can, but that'll hurt. I'd just as soon leave well enough alone."

"Not a very brave soul, are you?"

Christiana lowered her eyes again, unable to meet his gaze. "Let's just say that I have a low threshold of pain, and right now shoulder-high is it."

He straightened her blouse and buttoned it. His long fingers were warm against the base of her throat and sent a shiver down her spine. "At least nothing seems to be broken." Dillon picked up the camera lying on the ground next to her and examined it. "Except this."

Christiana took the camera from him and looked at the shattered lens. "Oh, no," she said softly. "I paid more than a thousand dollars for this, used." She checked the rest of it. "Oh, well, at least the camera itself seems to be all right."

"Is taking pictures a hobby of yours?" he asked as he put his jacket over her shoulders.

"You could say that." He didn't need to know that she'd had two books of photographs published.

He got to his feet and pulled Christiana to hers. She swayed, just a little, dizzy from the swift movement.

The man put his hands at her slender waist to steady her. "I knew you weren't all right. I'm going to take you home with me and call a doctor."

"But . . ."

"No buts. As soon as you've been checked over, I'll take you wherever it is that you belong."

"Look," she protested, "I . . ."

Before she could say another word, he handed Christiana her sweater and picked her up in his arms. "Exactly where *do* you belong?" he asked, his face inches from hers. "You're certainly not from around here."

Christiana's entire body stiffened. "I'm from the United States."

"What brings you to Prince Edward Island at this time of year?"

She didn't have to say it. She could leave right now and it would all be over with. But the words tumbled out anyway.

"Apslyn Employment Agency sent me here to interview for a job as nanny to Dillon Austin's daughter."

"You're Christiana Stevenson?" he asked in surprise as he looked at her more closely.

"Yes."

"The agency told me to expect you sometime tomorrow."

"I don't like to be late."

"I guess not." He lifted her onto the horse in front of the saddle, then hoisted himself up behind her. "I'm Dillon Austin."

"So I gathered."

He put his arms around her to grasp the reins. Considering that he was out in the cold with no shirt on, he was wonderfully warm.

"Comfortable?" he asked.

She turned her head just a little until she could meet his eyes. "I was nearly assassinated by a horse. *This* horse. What do you think?"

Dillon laughed and shook his head. "You could at least try to kiss up a little bit if you want the job."

But she didn't want the job. She desperately didn't want the job.

Christiana felt the muscles in his legs tense as he pressed his knees against the horse. He kept the animal's pace slow in an attempt to jar his passenger as little as possible. When they came to the fence Christiana had climbed earlier, he reached down from the horse to unlatch a gate, then closed it behind them. He approached the house from a different direction than the one Christiana had come from so they didn't get to go through her sanctuary. Instead, they rode through a shallow part of the lake to the other side, and then started up the hill to Lakecroft.

The dogs were already waiting for them on the veranda. They bounded down the steps and stopped, their tails wagging so hard the effort moved their entire bodies.

"What are their names?" she asked as Dillon climbed down from the horse.

"The one with the blue collar is Finn and the one with the black collar is Ian." He put his hands at her waist and gently lowered her to the ground. "You're not going to pass out on me, are you?" he asked, noticing how pale she suddenly seemed.

Christiana moved away from him, unable to bear his touch. "I'll be fine."

Dillon didn't believe her for a minute. "All right. Come with me."

She followed him up the steps and through the front door of Lakecroft. There was a small central hall with rooms radiating off from it and a staircase that led upstairs.

"There's a guest room up here you can use," Dillon said as he started up the stairs.

Christiana peeked into the living room and found herself surprised by the warmth and friendliness of its decoration. Again, it just wasn't what she expected of this man.

Once upstairs, Dillon opened a door for her and moved aside. Christiana stepped past him and found herself in a bedroom with a fireplace and a cozy four-poster bed with a down comforter as a spread and a handmade quilt folded neatly at the foot.

"You lie down," Dillon said, "while I call the doctor."

"I don't think I need a doctor."

"I'm going to call one anyway. Now do what I said and lie down."

Christiana handed Dillon his jacket and sat on the edge of the bed. Or rather sank onto it. There was nothing like a feather bed. "I suppose I've pretty much ruined my chances of getting the job, haven't I?"

Dillon looked at her for a long moment. "We'll talk about it later."

She watched him walk into the bathroom and heard the water running. When he came back out, he had a wet cloth in his hand.

"I said lie down. Don't you ever do what you're told without having it repeated?"

Christiana slipped off her shoes and slid back on the bed until her head touched the pillow. "I'm not used to having anyone tell me what to do."

Dillon pulled the quilt up, tucking it around her. Sitting beside her, still shirtless, he pushed her heavy hair away from her face and gently pressed the warm, damp cloth to the cut. "It isn't bleeding anymore."

Christiana's gaze moved over his handsome face. He seemed genuinely concerned about her.

"Would you like a fire to take the chill out of the air?"

"I don't want to be any more trouble to you than I've already been."

Dillon's eyes met and held hers. "All I have to do is light a match."

She wanted to pull her eyes away from his, but she couldn't. "Then thank you, yes. I'd like a fire very much."

He looked at her a moment longer, as though trying to discover what she was really thinking, then looked away as he placed the cloth over her forehead.

Christiana closed her eyes in relief. She'd never been very good at hiding her feelings or thoughts. Her eyes mirrored every emotion. Now her other senses took over. She felt Dillon rise from the bed and heard him cross the room. There was the scrape and hiss of a match being lit and the crackle of flames a few minutes later. She felt him standing near the bed looking down at her.

Without saying anything else, Dillon left the room, closing the door quietly behind him.

Christiana opened her eyes and stared at the door. Coming here had been a mistake. She should have gone with her own instincts and not allowed herself to be talked into this.

Taking the cloth from her head, she sat up slowly. Admittedly, she had a headache, but it wasn't anything she couldn't handle.

Rising from the bed, she made her way to the bathroom and turned on the light so she could look at herself in the mirror. It wasn't too bad—just some dried blood on her face and in her hair.

Leaning closer, she tried to get a better look at the cut. It was hard to see because her hair was in the way, but it didn't seem serious. Certainly not bad enough to bother a doctor about. Rinsing out the cloth, she cleaned her face, then went back into the bedroom to stand in front of the fire, her hands extended in front of her to catch the warmth. Whenever she'd imagined the perfect home, it had always included a bedroom with a fireplace.

Curiously, she went to the window and parted the drapes with the back of one hand so she could look outside. She smiled when she saw that she had a wonderful view of the lake—a lake, of course, being the other requirement for her perfect house. The red sunset splashed its colors across the water. She could hear the sound of the leaves rolling across the lawn as they were caught in the breeze.

It was utterly idyllic. For Christiana, who'd grown up privileged but in cities, this was a kind of life completely out of her realm of experience.

A movement below caught her eyes. A small man with a medical bag was walking around the house from the direction of the gravel driveway where her own car was parked.

Christiana took a final look at the sunset, then reluctantly let the drape fall back into place and made her way to the bed. She had to admit that it was something of a relief to lie down and close her eyes. The mild headache had turned into a throb.

She heard the front door close and the quiet sound of voices mixed with the crackle of the fire. There was a creak of wood as someone climbed the stairs. Again she heard the voices just outside her door and opened her eyes. Dillon stepped inside first. "Good. You're awake. The doctor's here."

The small man she'd seen arriving entered the room and flashed her a friendly smile. "I understand you had something of a run-in with Dillon's horse."

Christiana returned the smile. "That's certainly one way of putting it."

He turned on the light next to the bed and set his medical bag on a small table there. "Have you had any nausea?" he asked as he checked the wound.

She saw Dillon watching the proceedings over the doctor's shoulder. "No."

"Dizziness?"

"No."

"I thought she seemed dizzy right after it happened," Dillon said.

"All right," Christiana conceded. "I was a little dizzy, but it went away."

"Headache?"

"Yes."

"How severe?"

"That's a leading question to ask someone with a low threshold of pain. What's excruciating to me might be a minor inconvenience to someone else."

The doctor's lips twitched. "True." He removed a small flashlight from his bag. "Turn out the lamp, Dillon."

He did and the doctor shined his flashlight straight into Christiana's eyes. "Everything seems all right." He put the instrument back into his bag and Dillon turned on the lamp.

"What do you think?" Dillon asked.

"Well," the doctor said, straightening, "if she does have a concussion, it's a minor one." He turned his attention back to Christiana. "I'll give you something for the headache. If you start to feel some nausea, tell Dillon to call me. Otherwise, I don't think we have anything to worry about. Now, let's take a look at that other injury. Which shoulder is it?"

"Left," Dillon said.

The doctor slid her blouse over her shoulder and looked at it closely. "You've got some nasty bruising there. That's going to hurt for a few days." Gently lifting her arm, he raised it as high as he could without hurting her, and probed the area of the bruise with skillful fingers.

Christiana closed her eyes and gritted her teeth.

"Dillon, do you have a heating pad?" he asked.

"Just a hot water bottle."

"I guess that's better than nothing." He placed her arm on top of the quilt. "The medicine tablets I'm leaving for your head should also help with your arm, Miss Stevenson. I want you to make sure you take them."

"She'll take them," Dillon said.

"And make sure the water in the bottle is kept hot through the night."

"All right."

"I don't think I'll need to stop by again, but if either of you feels something is wrong, call and I'll get here as quickly as I can." He picked up his black bag.

"Thank you for coming," Christiana said.

"It was my pleasure. I'm just glad it was nothing more serious."

"I'll walk you out," Dillon said as he turned off the lamp and went with the doctor to the door. "Did you bring luggage with you, Christiana?" he asked, turning back to her.

"It's in my car."

"I'll bring it up for you. Do I need the keys?"

"It's not locked."

In a gesture that surprised her, Dillon came back to her and pulled the quilt up a little higher. His eyes looked into hers. "You look cold," he said quietly. He then left with the doctor.

Christiana stared at the door as it closed behind him, then closed her eyes and turned her head away. His kindness only made her more miserable.

And yet there were things she knew about him that told her Dillon Austin could be terribly cruel. Her thoughts drifted off....

She must have fallen asleep because the next thing she knew, Dillon was placing a hot water bottle on her shoulder. She opened her eyes and looked up at him.

Without saying anything, he handed her a pill and a small glass of water, then helped her into a sitting position. "This should help you get through the night without too many problems."

She swallowed the pill and handed back the glass. "Thank you."

Rising from the bed, Dillon walked to the fire and put on another log. "Are you hungry?" he asked. "I'm not the best cook in the world and my housekeeper has already left for the night, but I'm sure I could warm some soup or make some tea."

"No, thank you."

He crossed to the chair next to her bed and sat down. "While I was waiting for the water to heat for the hot water bottle, I went over the résumé sent by the employment agency."

She gazed up at him, already knowing what was coming. "And?"

"It says that you've taken care of only one child on a long-term basis."

"That's right."

"So you're not really a professional nanny. What makes you think you're qualified to take care of my daughter?"

"In your eyes, perhaps I'm not. I mean, I haven't attended any kind of professional nanny's school. But I love children and I've always been good with them. I have a lot of patience and have enough of the child left in myself to remember what it was like," she answered as honestly as she could.

"You'd rather be a nanny than a photographer?"

She was glad at that moment that the only light in the room came from the fire. "There are times when it's hard to earn a living with photography."

"I can imagine."

"Look," she said quietly, "I know that my qualifications are less than stellar, but I'm a good person and I'm genuinely fond of children. I think that if you'd just give me a chance you'd find that I'm ideal for the job."

Dillon looked at her for a long time before speaking. "All right. You have my okay. My daughter Katy is with my parents for the rest of the week. You'll meet her when she gets back. If she likes you, the job is yours."

Christiana honestly didn't know if she was glad or not. She'd certainly gotten what she'd come for. "Thank you."

He inclined his head as he rose from the chair. "You should try to get some more sleep."

"I will."

"I brought your luggage up while you were sleeping. It's next to the closet."

"Thank you."

"Is there anything you need from your suitcase?"

"No. I think I'll just sleep in what I'm wearing. At the moment, changing into a nightgown requires more energy than I can summon." Her eyelids were growing heavy.

Dillon pushed her hair away from her face. "I'll be back to check on you," he said quietly. "If you need me for anything in the meantime, I'll just be downstairs. I'll be able to hear you if you call."

"I'll be fine."

He looked at her for a moment longer, then left.

Christiana lay staring into the fire. Everything was falling into place, just the way her parents had planned it. She was here, in this house, with her dead sister's husband, and in a week, Paige's child would be here, as well.

Chapter Two

Christiana turned restlessly in bed, this way and that. Every time she dislodged the hot water bottle, the man in the chair beside her bed would replace it, then go back to his chair. He had a sheaf of music composition paper on his lap and a pen in his hand, but he couldn't concentrate on his work. He kept staring at the sleeping woman.

In the flickering light of the fire, he could see her pale, almost translucent skin; such a lovely contrast with her dark hair. Her lashes were long and shadowed semicircles on her cheeks. She was a beautiful woman in an understated way.

But it was more than her looks that intrigued Dillon Austin. It was Christiana herself. What was it he'd seen in her eyes when she'd looked at him that afternoon? There was no way to define it. He only knew he wanted to.

She said something in her sleep. Dillon leaned closer but couldn't make out the words....

"Thanks for picking me up, C.J."

Christiana had smiled at her sister Paige as she maneuvered her car through the light O'Hare International Airport traffic. The two women were complete physical opposites; one golden, one dark; one with brown eyes, the other blue. One was a famous model; the other preferred to work on the opposite side of the camera. "Just remember this the next time I need a ride at one in the morning."

Paige laughed, then sighed tiredly. "It's really good to be home."

"Mom and Dad have been excited for days. I know they have a big anniversary bash every year, but I think this one is really special for them because it's the first one that you and Dillon and Katy are coming to."

Paige didn't say anything, but Christiana attributed her silence to tiredness.

"Oh, and wait until you see what they've done with the spare bedroom. It has to be nothing short of a baby's vision of paradise. Mom hired a decorator to do it months ago and he just finished last week."

"It sounds nice."

"Is Dillon bringing Katy with him when he comes?"

She didn't say anything.

"Paige?"

"He's not coming," she said quietly.

Christiana glanced quickly at her sister's profile. "What are you talking about? I thought you said that he'd be able to get away from this tour he's been on long enough..."

"He couldn't work it into his schedule after all. It's that simple. And Katy's not coming, either. She's with Dillon."

"Oh, no, Paige. That's terrible. Mom and Dad have really been counting on this. You said just two days ago that they were coming."

"Things happen," she replied casually.

Christiana slapped her hand against the steering wheel. She couldn't bear to think of how this was going to hurt their parents. "This is ridiculous. In the nearly three years you've been married, none of us have met your mysterious husband."

"Dillon is a very private person."

"How can you spend fifteen years writing music and playing keyboards for one of the best bands in the world and be a private person?"

"Dillon's different."

Christiana let that pass as she stopped the car at a red light and turned to look at her sister. "This is going to break their hearts, you know. Katy is two and Mom and Dad haven't seen her since right after she was born."

"I'll explain things to them," Paige said expressionlessly. "They'll understand. They always do."

"Maybe that's part of the problem," Christiana said under her breath. The light changed and she drove through the intersection. "I'd like to explain a few things to your Mr. Wonderful."

"No!" Paige said sharply.

Christiana looked at her curiously. She knew that tone. "All right. What's really going on here, Paige? It's obviously a lot more than what you've told me so far."

Paige had been staring out the window. Now she turned slightly in her seat so she could look at her sister. "Dillon's having an affair."

"What?"

"It's not the first one he's had since our marriage and I'm certain it won't be the last, but that's why he isn't coming to the anniversary party. He'd have to give up his girlfriend for a few precious days."

Christiana stopped at another red light and turned to her sister in disbelief. "And you left poor little Katy with a jerk like that? What were you thinking?"

"No. I lied about that. I left her with her nanny. I just couldn't bear to be around her. Every time I look at her I think of Dillon."

"But what about Mom and Dad? They would have happily taken care of her."

"I need them for myself this weekend a hell of a lot more than Katy does."

Christiana was used to Paige's insensitivity, but that comment shocked her. Even so, she didn't remark on it. "Why don't you just divorce the man if he makes you so miserable?"

Paige took a cigarette out of her purse. A match hissed and flared in the darkness. "Oh, he'd like that. But I won't give him the satisfaction. He's mine and I'm going to keep him."

Silence fell between the sisters.

"I love him, you know?" Paige said quietly.

Christiana studied her sister's profile in the light of the streetlamps. "It sounds more like obsession than love."

Paige glared at her. "And what exactly do you know about either of those things, dear sister?"

"That was a cheap shot, Paige."

"You're right," Paige said quietly. "I guess I'm just tired. And maybe a little jealous."

"Jealous? Of what?"

"You. You're always so centered. Nothing ever throws you. It was the same when we were kids. There were times when I wished I could be you."

Christiana smiled.

"That wasn't meant to be funny," Paige said huffily.

"It's the irony that's amusing. I used to wish I could be you."

"You're kidding."

"Honest. Mom and Dad were always so openly affectionate with you. I was sort of tolerated by them. The three of you made a tight little unit that I was never able to completely penetrate."

"I never noticed."

The light changed and Christiana pulled out.

She was halfway through the intersection before she saw the other car bearing down on her passenger side, and by then it was too late. It roared drunkenly through the red light and smashed broadside into her car.

There was a terrible wrenching noise of metal crushing metal and glass shattering.

And then silence...

The first thing Christiana noticed was that she was breathing. She could feel the movement of her chest. The smell of gasoline hung heavy in the night air. Lights flashed. Voices shouted. Sirens could be heard in the distance.

Christiana opened her eyes and tried to get her bearings. She was stretched out on the pavement, her head cushioned by someone's jacket. A man knelt over her. "Just lie still," he said. "An ambulance is on the way."

Christiana was slowly remembering. She rose up on her elbows. "Where's Paige?"

"Is that the woman who was with you?"

"Yes. Is she all right? Where is she?"

The man's gaze involuntarily moved to a flickering light a hundred yards away. Christiana's gaze followed. Flames had completely engulfed her car and the one that had crashed into it until they had fused into one giant fireball. "Oh, God, she's not still in there—is she?"

"I'm sorry," the man said. "We tried to get her out. There just wasn't any..."

Christiana struggled to her feet. "I've got to get her out! She'll die!"

The man rose as well and steadied her with a hand on her arm. "She's already dead. No one could survive that."

"No!" She pulled away from him and, propelled by adrenaline, ran toward the fire. "Paige!"

It took the man fifty yards to catch her.

"Let me go!" she screamed as she struggled against him.

"No. Just stop it. There's nothing you can do for her. She's dead."

"No!" she screamed over and over again as she crumpled to the ground....

"Christiana, wake up."

"No, no, no."

Dillon put his hand on her shoulder. "Christiana, it's a dream. You're having a dream. Wake up."

Her eyes flew open. She was looking right at Dillon but couldn't focus on him. All she saw were flames.

"It's all right," he said quietly, as he wiped the tears from her cheeks. "You're here with me and you're safe. Nothing's going to hurt you."

The image of the fire slowly died away, leaving only the man. She couldn't bear to look at him and turned her head away. Her breathing was still ragged. "I'm all right."

Dillon pushed the hair away from her damp cheek with a gentle stroke of his fingers. "Do you want to talk about it? Sometimes talking about a bad dream makes it seem less real."

Christiana pulled her face away from his touch and stared into his eyes. The man was stunned at the depth of the pain he saw. "Some bad dreams are only too real, and no amount of talking can ever make them go away."

Dillon looked at her for a long moment. Without saying anything, he pulled the quilt up around her and tucked it in once again. "If you change your mind, I'm a good listener."

Christiana shook her head. "I'm very tired."

Dillon rose from the side of the bed and settled into the chair. His eyes were fastened on Christiana. He couldn't look away, and he didn't want to. For the first time in his life, he found himself completely intrigued by a woman.

Leaning his head against the back of his chair, Dillon watched Christiana, trying to penetrate the mystery with which she surrounded herself. He was still watching when dawn came a scant hour later, and still yet when the dawn turned into full-fledged morning. It wasn't until he heard the housekeeper moving around downstairs that he stirred.

Leaving the bedroom, he quietly closed the door after himself and went downstairs to talk to her.

Christiana heard Dillon leave. She hadn't gone back to sleep. And all the time she was aware of his eyes on her, wondering if he could see through her pretense. Even after he'd gone, she didn't move, but lay there deep in thought.

Dillon found the housekeeper in the kitchen. "Morning, Stella."

She looked at him in surprise. "You're up early. Or haven't you been to bed yet?"

"I haven't been to bed."

"Because of work, or does it have something to do with the car parked in the drive?"

He poured himself a cup of coffee and sat down at the counter. "The car. I hired a nanny for Katy."

"That was fast."

"I know. There was just something about her."

Stella looked at him with interest. "Something about her that appeals to you or something about her that will appeal to Katy?"

"Both, I hope."

Stella handed him some toast. "Don't tell me it took you all night to interview her."

"No. I ran her down with my horse."

"What?"

"She's fine. Or at least she will be. She had a bit of a head injury and I didn't want to leave her alone."

"What's her name?"

"Christiana."

"That's beautiful."

"It suits her." He finished his coffee. "I'm going to go for a walk, Stella. Take Christiana up some breakfast and make sure she has everything she needs."

Stella smiled as she watched him leave. Dillon almost always seemed happy. She hadn't seen him like that for years.

When Christiana's door opened some time later, she turned her head to find a large woman of about sixty entering her room, carrying a breakfast tray. "Good morning," the woman said, beaming a friendly smile as she set the tray on the bedside table and propped Christiana up on her pillows. "I'm Stella, Dillon's housekeeper. He tells me that you're going to be taking care of Katy, but that first we're going to be taking care of you. How's the head this morning?"

Christiana liked the woman immediately and returned the smile. "Much better than it was yesterday."

"Good." Christiana set the tray on Christiana's lap.

"And the final decision on my employment rests with Katy. If she doesn't like me, I'm history."

"Oh, she'll like you. And you'll like her. She's a delightful child."

"I can't wait to meet her. Does she look more like her mother or her father?"

Stella pursed her lips slightly before crossing the room to open the drapes. "Katy looks like—Katy. I can't honestly say that she takes after her father in any way but her temperament. As she gets older she might develop some of those model features her mother had, but for the most part I'd have to say that she doesn't look like either of them."

"Does she have blond hair?" Paige had always taken great pride in her mane of bright blond hair.

"No. Little Katy is about the most carrot-topped redhead you could ever hope to see." Stella went back to Christiana and tapped the plate. "Now, come on. Stop asking so many questions and eat your breakfast. You probably slept more than you ate last night."

"You're right, but I wasn't really hungry anyway."

"Hmm. Perhaps you should spend at least one more day in bed."

"That isn't necessary. I feel fine, really. In fact, I'd like to do a little exploring, if that's all right."

"That's fine by me. I'm sure Dillon's going to be working in the music room, but other than that, you can go anywhere in the house you want."

"This is a beautiful old place. It's almost like something you'd see on a postcard."

"Yes, it is. It used to belong to his grandparents."

"I didn't know that."

Stella looked at her rather curiously. "There's no reason why you would." She eyed the plate. "You're still not eating, young lady."

Christiana nibbled on a strip of bacon and drank some juice. It was obvious that the housekeeper was going to be a wonderful source of information if she could just figure out the right way to ask the questions without sounding as if she was being too nosy. "How long have you worked for Mr. Austin?"

The housekeeper raised Christiana's suitcase onto a long bench, opened it and began putting the clothes away. "Almost fifteen years." She shook her head. "Sometimes I can't believe how quickly the time has passed. And before that I worked for his grandparents."

"So you traveled with him?"

"Oh, no, nothing like that. Until a few months ago when we all moved here, Dillon had a house in Colorado."

"I see."

Stella looked at her curiously. "You sound surprised."

"I had pictured him more as a hotel person."

"No, not Dillon. He stayed in them when he had to, of course, but he's always enjoyed having a home to come back to."

Christiana drank more juice. "Did you know his wife well?" she asked casually.

"That one." Distaste rang in every syllable. "I knew her as well as I wanted to," Stella said firmly as she put a stack of clothing into a drawer. "And if you don't mind a little friendly advice, I wouldn't ask too many questions about the late Mrs. Austin if you want to keep your job."

"Why not?"

"Because there are some things best left forgotten, and she's one of them."

"But what about Katy? If she doesn't have questions about her mother now, she surely will as she gets older."

"Katy spent so little time with her mother that she doesn't miss her. If and when Katy wants to know about her mother, I'm sure Dillon will manage to treat Paige's memory with more kindness than the woman deserves."

Christiana felt as though she'd been slapped. Hard. Words in defense of her sister bubbled up inside her, but she couldn't say them aloud.

The housekeeper finished the unpacking, closed the suitcase and turned to Christiana. "Do you want to take a bath or shower this morning?"

"A shower."

"All right. There are towels and anything else you might need already in the bathroom. If you want me for anything, I'll be working around the house."

"Thank you, Stella."

The housekeeper lifted the tray from Christiana's lap and smiled at her. "Don't be so serious."

Christiana returned her smile. Despite what she'd said about Paige, it was impossible not to.

"That's better."

As soon as Stella left, Christiana got out of bed, slipped out of her clothes and climbed into a hot shower. The water felt good as it sprayed over her back and ran down her legs.

At the moment, she wished more than anything that she'd never let her parents talk her into this deceit. She'd never been very good at lying, and yet here she was, living a lie for who knew how many weeks? How on earth was she going to get through it?

But she had to. Dillon was no fit parent. Paige had made that abundantly clear. The problem was proving it in court so that her parents could get legal custody of the little girl. It was the only way Christiana could make up Paige's death to them. Katy could never replace Paige in their affections, but she was a part of the daughter they no longer had, and they loved the little girl deeply for that very reason.

Christiana washed her hair, rubbing gingerly around the area of the cut. Her shoulder really wasn't very painful. She was aware of the bruise and there was a certain uncomfortable feeling, but it was livable. Then she rinsed herself off and stepped onto the thick carpeting. As soon as she was dried and dressed in jeans and a thick sweater, she left her room to look around.

The door to the room next to hers was open and Christiana stepped inside. It was obviously Katy's room. There was a small bed, just the right size for a child. One end of it was filled with stuffed animals. The walls had hand-painted clouds and rainbows. There were a white chest of drawers and open baskets of toys just low enough for a two-year-old to get into. A child-size round table and two chairs were set in front of the windows. Containers of finger paints sat ready, as well as a roll of slick finger painting paper.

Christiana leaned against the window frame and looked outside. Just below was a green turtle-shaped sandbox, a swing set and slide, and a tire on a rope hanging from an old, sturdy tree. A white picket fence enclosed the play area to keep a curious child from wandering off.

It was perfect. Ideal. Everything had obviously been well thought out by someone who cared very much for Katy. Perhaps Dillon's parents. Or even the last nanny.

With a sigh, Christiana went back to her room for her jacket and purse, then went outside and down the hill to the lake, unaware of hazel eyes watching her from the house. Near the bank, she found a wonderful thick-trunked tree, its limbs bright with fall leaves, and she sat beneath it.

For a long time, she just sat there, staring out at the water, watching the breeze rippling along its surface. Then, with a feeling close to dread, she took a packet of letters out of her purse that Paige had written over the past few years. Her mother had handed them to her just before Christiana had left for Prince Edward Island and told her to make sure she read them. It was the only way for her to get a true idea of what Paige had gone through at the hands of her husband in the years before her death.

She slipped the top envelope out from under the rubber band and stared at it for a long moment. Then she removed the letter and unfolded the elegant gray paper. Her heart caught at the familiar sight of her sister's handwriting....

Dear Mom and Dad,
Sorry I haven't written for so long, but I've been really busy. I just got back from St. Thomas where we shot a swimsuit layout. I'll send you a copy of the magazine when it comes out.

Now, for the really important news: I've met the man I'm going to marry. Of course, he doesn't know it yet, but he will soon. I've finally figured out the perfect way to convince him.

He's different from the other men I've been involved with. Even you'd like him, Dad! His name is Dillon. Isn't that a wonderful name?

I'm going to try to get him to come home with me the next time I have a few days off so you can see for yourselves. Give my love to C.J. and tell her I wish her good luck with her book.

Paige

Christiana's eyes scanned the letter a second time. When she was finished, she lowered it to her lap. Not only had Paige's Dillon not made it to Chicago to visit her parents on Paige's next few days off—he'd never made it at all.

She looked at the date Paige had written at the top of her letter. It was just a few weeks before Paige had called to tell her about the marriage. Paige must have worked fast. But then, when it came to getting something she really wanted, Paige had always worked fast.

Folding the letter, she put it back in the envelope and slipped it through the rubber band at the bottom of the stack.

A furry head bumped her arm. Christiana laughed when she saw the dog nuzzling her. "Hello, there. Which one are you?" She saw the blue collar. "Finn, right?"

"Right."

She looked up to find Dillon standing over her.

"I saw you leave the house earlier. When you didn't come back, I thought I should check on you."

"I'm fine," she said quietly. "You don't need to worry about me." She inconspicuously slipped the letters back into her purse. "It was such a beautiful day that I wanted to spend some of it outside."

Finn quickly wriggled between them as Dillon sat on the ground next to her.

"Stella told me that this farm used to belong to your grandparents."

He nodded as he gazed out at the lake. "I spent a lot of time here as a child."

"That must have been nice."

"It was. I think those days are among my happiest memories. I didn't realize just how important this place was to me until after Katy was born, and by that time the farm had been sold."

"You were lucky to get it back."

"Luck had nothing to do with it. Money did."

Christiana shook her head. "I can't imagine parting with this place for any amount of money."

Dillon looked at her and then looked away. "People will sell anything if the money's right."

"That's cynical."

"Just an honest observation."

Christiana gazed at his profile. It was straight and clean. "Why did you hire me?" she asked suddenly. "There must have been more qualified people who applied."

"There were."

"So why me?"

"I think you're the one Katy would have chosen."

"What happened to the nanny she had before?"

"Katy's mother hired her. I personally didn't like the woman. She stayed here with us for about a month, but would get hysterical every time Katy got a little dirt on her hands. Part of being a child living on a farm is getting dirty. She just couldn't seem to understand that.''

"So you fired her.''

"Let's just say that the relationship was mutually and most satisfactorily dissolved.'' He glanced at Christiana. "I hope you aren't put off by a little dirt.''

"Oh, no,'' she said softly.

"And what about the isolation?''

Christiana shook her head. "I loved this place the moment I saw it,'' she said truthfully. "I've always wanted to live in a house by a lake, but I never had a clear vision of the house until now.''

"In the middle of nowhere?''

"Preferably.''

"Why's that?''

She lifted her shoulders in a delicate shrug. "Perhaps because I've never minded my own company. Why do you like it here?''

"Perhaps, like you, I enjoy my own company. But I don't think I could be happy in just any small town. There's something about this place that drew me to it when I was a child and still has a hold on me as an adult. Life here is the way life was meant to be: simple and clean. The people are honest and hardworking. There are no deceptions and no games. Being here is almost a cleansing of one's soul. You learn to trust again.''

Christiana lowered her eyes. He was here, in this beautiful place, learning to trust again, and she'd invaded his home bringing her lies with her. She would taint everything and everyone she touched here. That had never happened to her before and it would be difficult to live with, even for a short time.

"What's wrong?" Dillon asked. "You look as though you've lost your best friend."

She gazed out at the lake. "I love this place, but I don't belong here."

Dillon placed his finger under her chin and turned her face to his. "I know something's troubling you, Christiana. But being here will help. I know that from simple experience."

She looked into his eyes, hating herself for being so drawn to him. This man had been her sister's husband, and from all accounts, not a very good one. "And what if being here is part of the problem?" she asked quietly.

"Then, first you'll have to find peace within yourself."

Christiana turned her head to look at the lake.

"You're a strange woman, Christiana Stevenson."

"Strange, how?"

Dillon rose, then pulled Christiana to her feet. "You're beautiful," he said as he placed his finger under her chin again and raised her face so that he could examine it more closely, "but you haven't let that fact become the driving force of your life the way so many beautiful women do."

Christiana backed a step away from him. This was probably how he'd charmed Paige. "Thank you."

"Are you afraid of me?"

"Of course not," she said quickly. "Why would you even ask that?"

"Just an impression I get. I can almost feel your heart pounding from here."

Her heart *was* pounding. She could hear it in her ears.

"Let's go back to the house." He picked up her purse and handed it to her, then put his hand under her arm in a gesture that was nothing more than gentlemanly as they crossed the lawn together and climbed the hill to Lakecroft.

Chapter Three

"Dillon!"

Dillon and Christiana turned to find a man and woman walking toward them through the pasture. Finn and Ian both ran out to greet them.

"We were hoping you'd be home," the man said as they drew closer. His eyes came to rest appreciatively on Christiana. "And who's this lovely creature?"

Christiana smiled and extended her hand. She didn't know why she automatically liked the man, but she did. "I'm Christiana Stevenson."

His brown eyes twinkled. "Nice to meet you, Christiana. I'm John Bailey, and this woman standing beside me ready to kick my shin, at great personal risk to herself, is my wife, Leslie. We're Dillon's neighbors."

Leslie, a pretty woman who was about Christiana's height, rolled her brown eyes and flashed Christiana a warm smile. "Are you Katy's new nanny?" she asked.

"Only if she approves of me."

"Nothing like a little performance pressure, eh?" Leslie asked with a laugh.

"We were just going inside to have lunch," Dillon said. "Do you two want to join us?"

"I thought you'd never ask." John rubbed his hands together in anticipation. "What's Stella fixing today?"

Leslie looked at Christiana and sighed. "This is so embarrassing. The man doesn't have a subtle bone in his body. He lives for Stella's cooking. I think he'd marry her if she'd have him." She looped her arm through Christiana's and headed up the steps and into the house while the men brought up the rear. "How long have you been here?"

"Just since yesterday."

"So you haven't really had much time to explore our little island?"

"I think she's done enough exploring for a while," Dillon said. "I nearly ran her down yesterday with my horse."

"You nearly run everyone down with your horse." Leslie leaned closer to Christiana. "John and I have known Dillon since we were all kids. He rode the same way back then—all out. I can still see my father shaking his fist as Dillon shot by on—" She turned to Dillon. "What was your horse's name when you were a kid?"

"Archibald."

Leslie looked at him as though he'd lost his mind. "Archibald? Who on earth came up with that one?"

"Your father, as a matter of fact. He's the one who sold him to my grandfather."

"As I was saying. Great name for a horse."

"Don't mind my wife," John said as he put his arm around Leslie's shoulders. "She's always sticking her foot in her mouth. It's part of her charm." He smiled with genuine affection at Leslie. "At least, I've always thought so."

Stella heard them in the hallway and put her hands on her ample hips as soon as she saw John. "It's you again. I should have known you'd show up for lunch." Her voice was stern but her expression was amused.

Unrepentant, John kissed her rosy cheek. "What are you serving today, Stella? Something magnificent, I hope."

"Sandwiches."

"Oh, Stella, Stella, Stella," he groaned, crestfallen. "Sandwiches? Really?"

"Freshly baked, juicy glazed ham on thick slices of home-baked bread."

John brightened. "That's a little better."

"And vegetable soup."

"Is it anything like that incredible soup you served a few weeks ago?"

"One and the same."

He kissed her cheek again. "Thank you, dear lady. And if you ever decide to leave this dump, you can always work for me." He turned to his wife. "See, Leslie, I told you it would be worth the walk."

"And to think I actually thanked his mother after our wedding when she told me that John was now all mine," Leslie said to Christiana. "Such incredible naïveté."

As Christiana laughed, she caught Dillon's eye. Her smile quivered, then faded.

"That's the first time you've laughed since you got here," Dillon said quietly.

"Getting run over by huge horses seems to knock the humor out of most people I know," Leslie said dryly.

Dillon's eyes were still on Christiana, but she was looking everywhere but at him.

"Where are we eating?" asked John.

"I set things up in the library," Stella said. "There's a nice fire in there to take the chill off."

Christiana followed everyone into a friendly room with comfortable couches and chairs, including a wonderful old rocker placed just to the side of the big, old-fashioned stone fireplace. Two places had been set on the round coffee table. Stella bustled in and set two more places, then returned a minute later with a kettle of steaming, thick soup and a plate full of sandwiches.

John ladled some soup into his own bowl.

Stella watched him do it, then shook her head and muttered to herself as she left the room.

Dillon politely filled Leslie's and Christiana's bowls and then his own.

"Are you trying to make me look bad?" John asked as he passed the plate of sandwiches.

Leslie lifted an expressive brow. "You do that all on your own, darling. Don't try to spread the credit around."

It was impossible not to like these two, thought Christiana.

"Where's Cameron?" Dillon asked.

"Spending the day with my dad." Leslie turned to Christiana. "Cameron is our son. He and Katy are the same age. Almost the same age, anyway. Cam is a few weeks older." She turned back to Dillon. "He really misses Katy."

"I'll call you when she gets back so you can bring him over to play."

"I imagine she's been a tremendous comfort to your poor parents."

Dillon nodded, then changed the subject, leaving Christiana to wonder what they meant. Paige was the one who was dead. Why would Dillon's parents need comforting?

She glanced up and caught him looking at her. Their eyes held for a moment, then they both looked away. Christiana wished she felt more comfortable around him. It would make everything so much easier. She couldn't tell what he was thinking, and she was afraid that he could all too easily read her own thoughts.

Leslie watched the two of them for a moment, then she elbowed John and inclined her head toward Dillon and Christiana. He watched them for a few seconds between bites, then looked back at his wife and shrugged.

She sighed. The man didn't have a romantic bone in his body—unless raptures over a good meal counted. "Have you been a nanny long?" Leslie asked Christiana.

"I'm not really a nanny now. At least not a professionally trained one."

Leslie found that interesting. "What did you do before you got this job?"

"Photography."

"That's what she was doing yesterday when I ran her down," Dillon said. "I broke her camera lens."

"Oh, Dillon, you didn't," Leslie said.

"I'm afraid so. Which reminds me of something. Excuse me for a moment." He got up and left the room.

"What kinds of things did you photograph? Did you have a studio?"

Christiana's eyes followed Dillon until he disappeared from sight. "No," she said, forcing her attention back to Leslie. "I started out taking pictures to illustrate travel pieces, then moved on to simply taking pictures that interested me and trying to sell them on their own merit."

"Were you successful?"

"I'm now in child care," Christiana said with a smile. "What does that tell you?"

Leslie looked at her curiously. "Not a lot. Still waters run deep and all that. Do you have any family?"

"Just my parents."

"Where do they live?"

"Arizona." That was currently true. They spent their winters in Arizona and their summers in Chicago.

"Any brothers or sisters?"

Christiana hesitated before answering. "I had a sister. She died recently."

"Isn't that a tragic coincidence?" Leslie said, wide-eyed. "Dillon's sister died recently, as well."

"She did?"

"Poor Anne. Such a sweet woman. She had cancer. What did your sister die from?"

"An accident."

"For heaven's sake, Leslie," John said in exasperation. "Will you stop giving the poor woman the third degree and let her eat her lunch in peace?"

She flashed Christiana a charmingly apologetic smile. "I'm sorry. It's just that I like you, and when I like someone, I want to know all about them."

"It's all right," Christiana said, returning her smile, and privately wishing she'd met this nice woman under different circumstances. They might have become good friends.

Dillon returned with a large box that he handed to Christiana. "I felt bad about what happened to your lens, so I called a store in town and had one sent over this morning. It's not exactly what you had, but it's as close as I could come on short notice."

Christiana opened the box and removed the leather pouch, then took the lens out and examined it. "Oh, no," she said as she looked up at him. "I can't accept this. It's a much better lens than the one that was broken. Besides, the accident was partially my fault for being where I shouldn't have been in the first place."

"I'm afraid you're stuck with it. You see, it was on sale, so I can't return it. Just consider it an apology."

Their eyes met and held. "Thank you, Dillon. That's very kind of you."

"You're welcome." He looked at her for a moment longer, then turned to John and Leslie. "I'm sorry to desert you folks like this, but I have to get back to work."

"We're the ones who should be apologizing," Leslie said, as she rose and kissed Dillon's cheek. "It seems like we're always barging in on you at mealtimes."

"I enjoy seeing you. It breaks up the day."

Leslie looked at him suspiciously. "I'm going to think about that one before I say thank-you."

John rose, as well, half a sandwich in his hand. "Are we leaving?"

"I am," Dillon said. "You and Leslie, however, are welcome to stay and finish your lunch." He turned his attention to Christiana. "I don't know if I'll see you at dinner or not. I may work straight through."

"All right. I'll be fine on my own." Christiana watched him walk away.

Leslie watched Christiana watching Dillon and smiled. This situation could turn out to be quite interesting. "May I call you Chrissie? Christiana is a beautiful name, but it's rather a mouthful."

"Chrissie's fine."

"Let's sit on the veranda, Chrissie. We'll let John eat until he drops."

As soon as Christiana rose, Leslie looped her arm through hers and they went out to the veranda. Christiana sat on the swing while Leslie lounged on the railing, her back resting against a narrow pillar.

"We have to enjoy this weather while we can. Once winter arrives, we spend most of our time indoors."

"Do you have a farm?"

She nodded. "Our land borders Dillon's. It's not a very big one, as farms go. Some fields, a few cows and horses. Enough to keep us busy."

Christiana gently pushed herself back and forth on the well-oiled swing. She would have given almost anything at that moment to have felt truly at peace. "I think that I could sit here forever very contentedly."

"I know what you mean. Lakecroft is one of the most beautiful places in Charpentier. In all of Prince Edward Island, for that matter. I'm glad Dillon was able to get it back into his family. Katy's going to have a wonderful time growing up here."

"Do you think she will? Grow up here, I mean. Once Dillon finishes what he's working on, won't he be moving on?"

"Oh, no. He may have to leave once in a while to perform, but nothing like the way he used to. He bought this place specifically for Katy."

"I'd think that he'd start to feel closed in here after the kind of life he's led."

"Not Dillon," Leslie said with a laugh. "Oh, no. It was the other life that was getting to him. In his heart, Dillon belongs here. He always has. Unfortunately for us, as his friends, and unfortunately for Dillon and his peace of mind, his talents have taken him elsewhere over the years. But little Katy brought him back home."

"Is he good with Katy?"

Leslie paused before she answered. "He's getting better. I don't think he knew what to do with her at first. They've only really been together for about eight weeks. Maybe seven. It's taken some adjustment on both of their parts."

"Why wasn't he with her before that?"

Leslie started to respond, then stopped. "It's not my place to say anything."

Christiana tried not to press too hard. She gazed out at the lake. The wind had picked up a little and the sky had grown darker. "Did you ever meet Katy's mother?"

"Paige?" Leslie's voice was carefully nonjudgmental. "She never came to the island, but John and I met her in Colorado when we were guests of Dillon's."

"What did you think of her?" She turned her head so she could see the expression on Leslie's face.

Leslie considered her words carefully. "She and Dillon couldn't have been more different in character. You see, Dillon is a man of depth and sensitivity. He has tremendous integrity. Paige was shallow and mean. I can still see her smile. It was perfect and beautiful—until you noticed her eyes. They never smiled. They never showed any kind of emotion. I honestly couldn't believe Dillon married her. At first I thought the attraction might have been purely physical, but that's just not like Dillon. He requires more than that of his friends and he'd certainly require more than that of his wife. It didn't make sense to me for a very long time. Of course later on, when the facts became known, everything became quite crystal clear.''

''What facts?''

Leslie turned her head and looked at Christiana with contrition in her expression. ''There goes my mouth again. Forget I said that. Dillon would murder me on the spot.''

Christiana wasn't about to forget it, but she would set it aside—for now. ''I'm sure his wife must have had *some* good points. How was she as a mother?''

''She gave birth. That's about the extent of it. Once Katy was born, Paige went back to pursuing her career—and other interests—as though the child didn't exist. She put on a good show whenever anyone was around, but she couldn't keep it up for long. Katy spent all of her time with nurses and nannies.''

''And where was Dillon while this was going on?''

''Dillon, by his own choice, stayed away from both Paige and Katy. He had his reasons, but now I think he regrets not being with Katy more.''

John came out of the house and took a deep breath of the crisp, fresh air. ''What are you two talking about?''

''Dillon and Paige,'' Leslie said.

''An interesting subject.''

"To say the least," his wife agreed. "Are you sated, you beast? Can we leave now?"

"We can. And may I say that Stella will be gratified by the fact that neither a crumb nor a drop is left."

Leslie looked at Christiana and raised her eyes heavenward. "Little does she know that she has John to thank almost entirely."

"Something tells me she does."

"I suppose you're right," Leslie agreed with a resigned sigh. "I'll call her to apologize later." As she rose from the railing, Christiana started to get up, as well. Leslie touched her hand. "Please, stay comfortable, Chrissie. I'll see you soon."

Christiana swung back and forth while she watched the two of them saunter off arm in arm and thought about what Leslie had said about Paige. She was strangely unoffended. Christiana had loved her sister very much, but she'd never been blind to her faults. For all of the promise of Paige's looks, for all of the charm she could turn on at will, there had always been something missing. She'd used people to get what she'd wanted all of her life, and they'd let her—Christiana included. The difference was that Christiana had known she was being used. Her parents never had. To them, Paige was everything wonderful. And now, especially, that's the way it should be. Whatever unpleasant things Christiana uncovered about Paige while she was here would remain her secret. She would never willingly tarnish her parents' memories.

One question still nagged at her, though. If Dillon was all of the things Leslie said he was, why did he ever marry Paige? And once he discovered that the marriage wasn't going to work out, why on earth hadn't he divorced her?

The front door opened and Stella stepped onto the porch. "I'm going. I forgot to remind Dillon earlier and he's probably forgotten by now that I'm leaving early today. It's my brother's birthday and I want to get to his house a little early to help with the party. You two are on your own for dinner. There's some soup left that I managed to hide from John. And some ham and bread if you're inclined."

"Thank you."

"See you in the morning, dear."

"Have fun."

Christiana heard her car start a few moments later. Leaving the veranda, she walked around the house. The grass was still green and immaculately manicured, though leaves were scattered across the short blades. Opening the white gate, she wandered through Katy's play area and went out the other side and down the hill toward the big white barn.

There was wonderful antique farm equipment in the old building, most of it horsedrawn, no doubt from the days of Dillon's grandparents. Fifty-year-old bikes hung upside down by their tires.

The aromas in the barn were wonderfully clean and country—the sweetness of the hay stored in bales on an upper deck, the strong scent of the old leather saddles hanging on pegs, even the smell of the horses who spent time there.

But what really interested Christiana was a long table with carpenter's tools neatly laid out. A rocking chair sat nakedly amid shavings, waiting for someone to finish his work. That surely couldn't have been left from decades earlier. She rubbed some of the wood shavings between her fingers. They looked fresh. Then she gently ran her fingertips over the rough, unsanded surface of the chair.

Could this be Dillon's handiwork? Christiana shook her head. The man was full of surprises.

Quietly thoughtful, she crossed back to the house. The skies had grown even darker with rain clouds. At least she hoped they were rain clouds. She wasn't ready for snow yet.

Finn and Ian were standing in the hallway waiting for her. As soon as she opened the door, they dashed past her and leaped from the veranda without bothering to use the stairs, running their own private race.

Smiling, she decided to wander through the rest of the house, starting in the library so she could look through the books. Taking a mystery from one of the shelves, she carried it tucked under her arm while she explored the more formal living room and dining room. There was a room with the door closed that was probably the music room where Dillon was working, and a family room that was probably where Katy spent most of her time. The kitchen had been completely modernized and contained all the latest equipment, but it had been done carefully, to retain the flavor of its old-world charm. Even the stone fireplace that took up most of one wall had been left intact and apparently was still functional.

Christiana had been here for just one day, but she loved it already. If she could have built the house of her dreams anywhere in the world, Lakecroft would have been the house and Prince Edward Island would have been the place.

With the book still under her arm, she started back toward the library with the intention of sitting in front of the fireplace, but she heard the dogs barking and let them in first. As soon as she opened the door, she could see that the wind had picked up considerably from before. It was still early, but the sky had grown almost black except for the lightning fingering its way across the horizon. It took a long time for the rumble of thunder to reach her ears.

Setting the book on a table, she stepped onto the veranda and stood staring out with one arm wrapped around a narrow white column. The wind whipped her hair into a frenzy, but she welcomed it. For weeks now since her sister had been killed, she'd wrapped herself in an unnatural calm. Inside, she felt more like this storm and it gave her something of a release just to be in it.

There was no small shower before the real rain started. The skies just opened with a vengeance, sending the water slashing to the ground. The earth was alive with the rumble of thunder.

Christiana stepped off the veranda and walked to the middle of the yard. Large drops hit her face with stinging force. Rather than shying away, she raised her face to meet them.

"Christiana!" Dillon yelled as he came up behind her. "What are you doing?"

She lowered her eyes as he drew closer to her. "It's wonderful, isn't it?" she yelled over the wind.

"Didn't your mother ever teach you to come in out of the rain?"

"She tried. What about yours?"

"She taught me to be a gentleman and rescue damsels in distress."

Lightning flashed overhead. This time the thunder was nearly simultaneous.

"That's a little too close," Dillon yelled, as he tapped Christiana's shoulder and pointed to the house.

"I'll race you!"

"What?" he asked in surprise.

"One, two, three." She took off running before "three" was out of her mouth. She flew across the yard and up the steps onto the veranda with Dillon a fraction of a second behind her.

Both of them were soaked to the skin and laughingly out of breath as they stood dripping in the foyer.

"Next time, I do the counting," Dillon said, as he pushed her wet hair away from her face.

"Oh, no. You have longer legs. I need some advantage."

Their smiles faded as they stood there looking at each other. "I've never met a woman who actually enjoyed this kind of storm," he said quietly.

Christiana could feel her heart beating. She wanted to put her hand over his to hold it on her hair. Instead, she stepped away from him. "I have ever since I was a child. I could never imagine anything as angry as a storm. There's something both frightening and compelling about it at the same time.''

"Well, next time, if there's lightning, admire it from a safe distance. I only do one rescue per season.''

Christiana's eyes sparkled. "You should see yourself. Your sweater's stretched three sizes.''

"I'll bill you for it. And before you go throwing stones, you should get a look at yourself.''

"I imagine we both look like a couple of drowned ducks.''

"Nothing nearly so nice.''

"I suppose we should change.''

"That would be the wise thing. Unless, of course, there's something about pneumonia that's always fascinated you, as well.''

A dimple hovered at the corner of her mouth, charming the man. "I'll see you later.''

Dillon's eyes followed her up the stairs. She was most definitely a woman of contradictory moods. Life with her in the house would never be boring.

When Christiana got to her room, she closed the door and leaned her back against it. Coming here had seemed such a simple thing. Was it really only yesterday?

Still wet, Christiana went to her window and held the curtains back with her hand. Lightning flashed over the lake. But it wasn't the lightning or the lake that she was seeing. It was her mother's face.

They'd been sitting in the living room of her parents' Chicago condominium. Paige had been dead less than six weeks.

"I want Katy," her mother had said, her once youthful face drawn and tired with grief. "It's not right that a man who treated our daughter so badly should be allowed to raise our granddaughter. It's just not right."

"He's her father," Christiana had said quietly. "He has legal custody. There's nothing you can do about that." She thought for a moment. "Perhaps you could convince him to give you and Dad visitation rights."

"I don't want her to visit. I want her to live here. She's all we have left of our Paige, and I don't want her brought up in the kind of environment this man undoubtedly provides. A rock musician! Can you imagine what that child's life must be like?"

"Mom...."

"I understand that this Dillon person is looking for a nanny for Katy."

"How did you find that out?"

"A private detective. I even know which employment agency he's using."

Already Christiana didn't like the sound of where this was leading.

Her mother had looked at her with such hopeful eyes. "I want you to go to this agency and apply for the job."

Christina had been surprised—and yet not surprised at all. "But, Mom, they'll check my references. I have none," she said reasonably.

"I've already explained the situation to some friends of ours. They're willing to vouch for you."

"And what about my name?"

"You can go by Christiana. I'm sure that when Paige spoke of you to this Dillon person, she called you C.J., just as she always did. And for your last name, just drop White and use your middle name. You'll be Christiana Stevenson."

Christina had looked at her with quiet resignation. "You've already got this worked out, don't you?"

"I've given it a lot of thought, if that's what you mean."

"And what is it that I'm to do if—and it's a big if, Mom—I get this job as Katy's nanny?"

Her mother had taken her hand between her own. "You're to keep your eyes and ears open. I want a record of every move this man makes. You'll become our eyewitness to the kind of man he is. You'll be able to testify against him in a custody hearing. No judge would allow a man like that to raise a child."

"And what if he's a good father?"

"You know what Paige said about him. He has no more interest in being a father to Katy than he had in being a proper husband to Paige." Her mother's eyes had filled with tears. "It breaks my heart when I think of what he put our poor baby through." Her mother had patted Christiana's hand. "Honey, I know this goes against your nature, but you must think about what's best for Katy. Paige is no longer here to do that, so we must do it for her."

And that was the crux of the matter. Paige had died a horrible death and Christiana had survived. Though they never said anything, Christiana wondered if her parents would ever forgive her for that. She wondered if she'd ever forgive herself. All she could do now was try to make it up to them as best she could.

"If I do do this, Mother, it has to be with the understanding that I report exactly what I see. If Dillon Austin is a good father, that's what I'll report back to you."

"Fair enough. But that isn't what you'll find...."

A loud clap of thunder brought Christiana back to the present.

She wished to heaven she'd never let her mother talk her into this. It wasn't right. She rubbed her tired eyes. She didn't want dinner. She didn't want anything but sleep.

Chapter Four

Christiana sat straight up in bed. Her heart was pounding so hard she thought it was going to fly out of her chest.

She wrapped her arms around herself and began rocking back and forth, trying to numb the pain. When that didn't help, she grabbed her pillow, buried her face in its softness and screamed until she couldn't scream any longer. She couldn't take one more night of that horrible dream. That horrible reality.

She lay down, still clutching her pillow and stared at the ceiling, waiting for her heartbeat to get back to normal. Everything was quiet. The thunderstorm had stopped.

"I'm so sorry, Paige," she whispered hoarsely into the darkness.

Christiana lay there for a long time, unable to sleep, unwilling to try. The book she'd gotten from the library earlier was still downstairs on the hall table. Her purse with Paige's letters was in the library. It was only three in the morning and Christiana had to do something to occupy herself, so she climbed out of bed and padded barefoot across her room to the door. The lights were all out upstairs, but she could see a dim light coming from somewhere downstairs.

Still in her long cotton nightgown, she tried to go quietly down the steps, but they creaked beneath her. She winced at the noise, and wished them silent as she carefully continued. She saw the book in the dim light and picked it up, then went into the library. The fire had burned itself out, but the embers still glowed orange. Her purse was next to the couch where she'd left it at lunch. She had to remember to be more careful with her things. Particularly those concerning Paige.

Christiana started to go back to her room, but then she saw a light coming from the music room. Setting her things on another table, she walked to the partially open door, pushed it open a little more and looked inside.

It was a big room, bare except for a grand piano and a fireplace. Dillon sat at the piano, a score sheet spread out in front of him, a pen in his hand as he quickly jotted the notes to music that only he could hear.

He looked up and stared into the fire for a moment. His long fingers moved in the air as though playing the music, and he wrote some more.

She watched Dillon for a long time, her photographer's eyes missing nothing. He'd changed from his wet clothes into jeans and a dry sweater with the sleeves pushed up to his elbows. Her eyes moved over his strong forearms to his hands.

His hands. They were big, to match his own size, with long fingers that were perfectly shaped for playing a piano. They were hands that a person could trust, belonging as much to an artist as they did to a carpenter. They were hands that a woman would notice—and daydream about.

But more than that, as she watched him now, she thought back to some of the music he'd written over the years. Christiana had been drawn to the music long before she'd known who composed it. The people who sang the songs got most of the fame and credit, not those who wrote them.

To her, Dillon's music had always been larger than life, filled with symphonic sounds that simply weren't heard with any other groups. Now she stood in a doorway, watching him create. She wondered what kind of remarkable mind could hear such beautiful sounds and put them on paper so that others could hear them, too.

She suddenly felt as though she were intruding on something very private and started to close the door, but Dillon saw the movement.

"Christiana?"

She reluctantly opened it again, an embarrassed smile touching her mouth. "I'm sorry. I saw the light. I didn't mean to disturb you."

"It's all right. You're not disturbing me at all. I can use the break." He tossed his pen down and stretched his long frame. "What time is it?"

"After three." She moved farther into the room and looked at what he'd been writing. "What are you working on?"

"Something just for myself."

"You mean that no one else is going to get to hear it?"

Dillon's eyes moved over her as she leaned over his music. Her nightgown was charmingly old-fashioned, giving nothing away of the slender curves of her body beneath its voluminous folds. It was very enticing.

"I mean that this work may have no commercial value at all. It's just something that I've wanted to write for a long time, and now I can afford to."

"Classical?"

"In the sense that it's intended to be played with a symphony orchestra, yes. How did you know?" he asked curiously.

"Your music has always leaned in that direction."

"I suppose it has. I don't know whether it's been my curse or my gift that I've always heard the piano music I write with full accompaniment."

"Will you play something for me?"

"Anything in particular?"

"What you were just writing."

"It isn't finished."

"It doesn't matter. I'd just like to hear what was going on in your mind while I was watching you."

He looked at her in surprise. "All right."

Christiana sat cross-legged on the floor, her nightgown falling into a white circle around her.

Dillon had unfolded the score sheet like an accordion while he'd been writing. It covered the entire width of the piano. He now folded it and set it directly in front of him.

With the first few notes, Christiana felt her heart catch. She folded her hands in her lap and closed her eyes as she listened, transported. He played for perhaps three minutes, then stopped.

Christiana's eyes flew open. "What's wrong?"

"That's it. That's all there is of this song. What did you think?"

"I think it's exquisite," she said softly. "I want it to go on and on."

"I wish all music critics were as kind as you."

"Kindness has nothing to do with it."

Dillon pushed his music aside. "I think I'm going to give it up for tonight. What are you doing down here, anyway?"

She got to her feet. "I couldn't sleep, so I came downstairs for a book."

"Are you hungry?" he asked.

She thought for a moment. "Yes, as a matter of fact, I am. What about you?"

"Starving. We could run a raid on the kitchen."

"Stella told me before she left that there was some soup in the refrigerator. And leftover ham."

"Sounds good." Dillon rose from the piano. "Let's go." He put his hand on the small of her back and guided her out of the music room, down the hall, and into the dark kitchen. "You get the soup out of the refrigerator," he said as he flipped on the lights, "and I'll get the pan to warm it in."

Christiana crossed to the refrigerator. "Here it is." She removed a covered glass casserole and carried it to the butcher block island.

Dillon ladled the soup into a pan and turned on the gas burner. "How are you at slicing bread?"

"I still have most of my fingers."

He grinned at her. "There should be a bread knife somewhere in there," he said, pointing at a big black block of wood that had the handles of eight knives showing.

Christiana found it on the third try. "Ta da," she said with a smile, holding up the bread knife.

"Good girl. Now, you'll find the bread on the counter behind me in the wooden bread box."

She found a loaf of freshly baked bread and carried it to a cutting board on the counter. "Thick or thin slices?"

"Definitely thick."

She cut off two slices while Dillon ladled the hot soup into two earthenware bowls.

"With ham or without?"

"Without. Do you mind sitting at the island instead of at the table?" he asked.

She shook her head.

He put the bowls on plates he'd already arranged on the island so that she was sitting at the long end of the L and he was close beside her at the short end of the L. "I'm going to have a glass of wine. Would you like one?"

"Yes, thank you," Christiana said, as she sat down and put the cloth napkin on her lap.

Dillon removed a bottle from a built-in wine rack, uncorked it, and poured them each a glass. "I know I should let it 'breathe' for a few minutes," he said as he set their glasses down and took his own seat, "but frankly, Christiana, it's been a long day and I'm tired. By the time the wine is finished breathing, I plan to be asleep." He raised his glass in a toast. "Welcome to Prince Edward Island in general, and to Lakecroft in particular."

Her eyes on his, Christiana gently clinked her glass to his and sipped the smooth red wine.

"Now," he said, picking up his spoon and starting on his soup, "You know a lot about me and I know very little about you—other than the fact that you have impeccable taste in music."

Christiana's smile flashed.

"Who are you, Christiana Stevenson?"

She was so surprised by his question that she nearly choked on the soup. "Who am I?"

If Dillion noticed he gave no indication. "What kinds of thoughts do you have? What are your hopes and dreams and desires?"

"You don't want to know too much, do you?" she said with a laugh.

"Only everything." He studied her lovely face. "What makes Christiana tick?"

She got a faraway look in her eyes and shook her head. "Boy, if I knew the answer to that, I'd be a happy woman."

"Are you unhappy?"

Her eyes met his. "Sometimes. Isn't everyone?"

"There are degrees," he said quietly. "Deep in your eyes, even when you're laughing, I can see that there's something haunting you so that you're never quite completely happy."

Christiana lowered her eyes. "Then you see more than most people do."

Dillon reached across the table and placed his index finger under her chin. "Look at me."

She did.

He gazed into her eyes for a long time. "With you, I think I do. Is it anything you can talk about?"

She shook her head, wishing with all her heart that she could have confided in him.

Dillon released her.

"I can tell you that part of my problem is that there are people counting on me. But no matter what I do, someone is going to get hurt."

"This involves your family, doesn't it?"

"How did you know?"

Dillon shrugged. "Dilemmas like that usually do."

Christiana looked at Dillon and shook her head.

"What?" he asked.

"I wasn't expecting to like you."

Dillon smiled at her with a warmth that took her breath away. "You sound as though liking me has come as a rather unpleasant surprise."

"Just a surprise." She lowered her eyes to the napkin on her lap, picked it up and folded it neatly before setting it next to her plate. She felt sick inside. "I'll just do these dishes and then go back to my room."

"Stella can do them when she gets here in a few hours."

"I don't mind," Christiana said as she rose and reached for his plate.

Dillon covered her hand with his. "Please leave them. Stella will be all over me if she gets here and finds no dishes to be done. She'll think we didn't eat and I'll never hear the end of it."

"All right," she said with a smile as she took her hand from his. "I'll just say good-night, then."

"Good night, Christiana. Try to get at least a little sleep."

"I will. Thank you for the snack."

Dillon watched her leave, then leaned back in his chair with a long sigh, his hands folded behind his head as he looked straight ahead. The more mysterious she was, the more determined he became. Something about her touched him inside and he couldn't ignore that.

Christiana found her book and purse and went to her room. She was losing perspective—or she was finding it. She didn't know which.

Turning on the bedside lamp, she pulled the packet of letters out of her purse. Sinking cross-legged into the middle of the feather mattress, she removed the top letter and unfolded it, then stopped and closed her eyes. She dreaded reading it, but she had to.

Opening her eyes, she began to absorb her sister's words, skipping over the small talk.

... There's something I must tell you, though I know you're both going to be upset. I married

Dillon Austin four weeks ago. I would have
loved having you at the wedding, but Dillon is
a very private person and refused to even consider inviting anyone.

As you can imagine, I, who've dreamed since
childhood of an elegant wedding with hundreds
of guests, was at first brokenhearted, but I love
him very much and want nothing more than to
make him happy. He has a very busy schedule,
so we haven't been able to spend much time together. I hope that changes eventually, but I
can't see that happening anytime soon....

Christiana sat staring at the words long after she'd
stopped reading. Would Dillon—the Dillon that she
was coming to know—have ridden roughshod over
the feelings of the woman he was supposed to have
loved, the way the Dillon in Paige's letter had? She
couldn't even imagine it.

She put that letter on the bottom of the small stack
and slid out the next one, dated a few weeks later.

...I'm going to have a baby! Dillon is something less than happy about it—I think he
wanted to have me to himself a little longer—but
I'm sure he'll adjust in time. He's still traveling
and doesn't want me with him, though I certainly wouldn't mind. We see each other so
rarely....

She pulled out the next letter, written months later.

...She's the most beautiful little girl. I'm nam-
ing her Katy. Dillon hasn't seen her yet. He
could have come home right after she was born,
but for some reason he didn't. Now she's two
weeks old and still hasn't met her father. Sometimes I wonder why he married me....

And the next.

...I enjoyed your visit. It's nice to know that
there's someone in my life who still cares about
me. Katy's now three months old and still hasn't
met her father. I've heard rumors that he's involved with one of the women who continually
chase after him. I guess I should have expected
it, but I really thought he loved me. I don't understand how he can just turn his back on the
two of us as though we don't exist....

Christiana stopped reading. This just wasn't right.
Paige came off in the letters sounding like the perfect wife and mother, and even if Leslie hadn't told
her otherwise, Christiana would have known it.
Nurturing wasn't something Paige had been capable
of doing. Accepting it, maybe. Offering it? Never.

Christiana rose from the bed and started to pace.
She was really torn. Obviously Paige had been miserable. But was that Dillon's fault or her own?

She wished desperately that she could talk to Dillon about this; to hear his side of it. But how could
she possibly initiate such a conversation with him?

He would tell her it was none of her business, and rightly so, then kick her out on her ear.

That left her with the problem of her parents. They—her mother in particular—believed everything Paige had told them over the years. And who knew what she'd said in phone conversations? She'd never be able to convince them of Dillon's basic decency because to do so meant they'd have to accept that Paige was a liar.

Walking to the window, Christiana stared out at the lake. The sun was rising in bright ribbons of color.

Her eyes moved to the dock and the lone man standing at the end of it with his hands in his pockets. She could feel his solitude as though it were her own. What was he thinking? What was he feeling?

As she watched, Dillon turned and looked toward the house. He'd somehow known she was there. Christiana didn't step back, but stayed where she was. After a moment, he walked back to the house. She heard the door close and then his footsteps on the stairs. They paused in front of her door.

Christiana walked quietly to the door and rested her hand on the cool wood. He was here on the other side. All she had to do was open it.

The footsteps moved on down the hall. Another door closed. Her hand fell to her side.

Christiana stripped off her nightgown and put on a clean pair of jeans, a sweater and a jacket. She had to get out of here.

Taking her camera and camera bag with all of her lenses, she went outside to the dock and climbed into the little skiff. It rocked so she sat down. Yesterday, she'd wondered how The Sanctuary would look at sunrise. Now she was going to find out.

She had never actually rowed a boat before, so it took her a few minutes to get the hang of it. But soon she was gliding along the lake, close to the bank.

The trees became more numerous, until finally she couldn't see through them at all. And then she was there, gliding through the silence around the trees growing out of the shallow water.

She put different lenses on her camera for different kinds of pictures.

The boat flowed along on the slow current. Every once in a while, Christiana had to push an oar against a tree trunk to avoid bumping into it.

Stretching out on the bottom of the boat, she lifted the camera to her eye and looked straight up. The sunrise was sending shafts of colored light streaming through the fall leaves. She took picture after picture, one lovelier than the next.

Then Christiana lowered the camera to her stomach and just gazed about her. The little boat stopped moving, and that was fine with her. She stayed where she was for another hour, not really thinking about any of the things that were bothering her, but trying to just absorb the beauty of the moment.

The sunrise ended. The Sanctuary was still beautiful—haunting, in a pleasant way. But Christiana knew she should be getting back to Lakecroft before she was missed.

Sitting up in the boat, she looked around. She'd come aground in mud. That frankly didn't seem like much of a problem. After putting all of her camera equipment away, she picked up one of the oars and with it, tried to push the skiff off the mud.

It didn't work.

She stood to get better leverage and used both oars. The skiff moved with a hard jerk to the right and knocked the oars out of her hand.

Swearing softly under her breath, Christiana kneeled in the bottom of the boat and stretched as far as she could. Her fingertips just brushed the wood of the oar closest to her.

She crept a little closer to the edge and stretched again. This time she touched a little more of the oar.

"All right," she said to herself, "just a little more." She deliberately tilted the little boat with her weight—not much. Just enough to give her an added inch of reach.

"Gotcha!" she said triumphantly as her hand closed around the oar. But at that moment, the boat wobbled precariously. Christiana lost what little balance her awkward position offered her and went spilling face first into the mud.

She just lay there for a full five seconds before pushing herself up and sitting in the mud next to the oars. She glared at them through mud-caked eyelashes. "I should just leave you both here," she told them as she struggled to her feet and picked them up. "It would serve you right." Squelching through the mud to the skiff, she threw them none too gently into the bottom.

After making sure that her camera equipment hadn't fallen out, she went to the front of the skiff and pushed hard to get it to move. The mud almost acted like a suction against the boat and wouldn't give it up without a fight.

When she finally managed to get it most of the way into the shallow water, she lifted her foot to climb in and her shoe got sucked off.

"Oooh!" she breathed in exasperation as she turned to retrieve the shoe—as though she'd ever be able to wear the stupid thing again.

Tossing her shoe into the skiff, Christiana followed after it. She rinsed the oars off in the water so she could use them, but couldn't see the point in doing the same with herself. The water had been so churned up by the storm the night before that it was almost as muddy as she was.

It took her fifteen minutes to get the skiff back to the dock. In the meantime, the mud had dried.

Picking up her sneaker in one hand and her camera bag in the other, she strode angrily up the hill and across the lawn. The only good thing at this point was that Dillon was probably still in bed and wouldn't see her.

No sooner had Christiana thought that, than she saw him sitting on the veranda, a cup of coffee in his hands. He caught sight of her at the same moment, and after his initial look of surprise, his eyes filled with laughter.

"Not one word," she warned him as she stormed past, slamming the door behind her.

Stella had been at the other end of the veranda, sweeping it off. She and Dillon looked at each other and laughed out loud. "I think I'm going to like having her around here," Stella said when she could finally talk. "She sure knows how to break up a day."

Chapter Five

"A little fortification before you start your walk back to Lakecroft," Leslie said, as she handed Christiana a mug of hot cocoa and sat next to her on the top step of the Baileys' porch.

"Thanks." She wrapped her hands around it for the warmth as she watched Ian and Finn patiently waiting for Cameron to finish petting them. "I don't think I've ever seen dogs as good-natured as these two."

"And smart," Leslie added. "Wait until you see the way they baby-sit for Katy. You'd think she was one of their puppies."

Christiana sipped the cocoa and sighed contentedly. "This is delicious. I haven't had cocoa with cinnamon in it since I was five."

"John likes it that way, too."

"John probably likes it any way you make it."

"True." She looked sideways at Christiana. "There's no reason for you to be so nervous about meeting Katy today, you know."

Christiana was chagrined. "Is it that obvious?"

"Only to someone who's gotten to know you rather well over the past week. She's just a little girl in desperate need of a mother figure, and she's going to love you."

"I hope so. I wish Dillon was going to be here, though."

"When's he due back?"

"Not until tomorrow. At least that's what Stella told me. I didn't get a chance to talk to him before he left, what with being covered in mud at the time," she said dryly. "By the time I was clean, he was gone."

"And you've missed him." Leslie's voice was tinged with a certain satisfaction.

"Well, I've been in the house alone every night except for Finn and Ian. It's been a little lonely."

"I'll bet." Her tone was filled with unmistakable meaning.

"Oh, Leslie, come on," Christiana said in exasperation. "Stop trying to invent a relationship where there isn't one. You've been doing that all week."

"But you just said that you missed Dillon!"

"No, I didn't. I said that I'd been a little lonely because there was no one but the dogs and me in the house at night. That's a generic kind of loneliness, not a desperate romantic longing for one man in particular."

Leslie wrinkled her nose. "Oh, I'm sorry, but it goes against my nature to mind my own business. The first time I laid eyes on you, I knew that you and Dillon were meant to be together. You've no idea how frustrating it is to be so sure about something when you can't convince anyone else."

Christiana stared into her cocoa.

"At least admit that you're attracted to him."

She thought of Dillon standing with her in the foyer, his warm hand pushing her wet hair from her face as his eyes looked into hers. "Of course I'm attracted to him. What woman wouldn't be? That doesn't, however, mean that I intend to do anything about it," she said firmly as she finished the cocoa and handed Leslie the empty mug. "I'd better leave now if I want to be at Lakecroft when Katy gets there."

"Let me know how things go."

Christiana kissed her on the cheek. "I will. Thanks."

As soon as she got up, Finn and Ian started wagging their tails. There was nothing they liked better than a good run, and they'd already recovered from the one on the way over. The three of them struck out across the pasture. Christiana started walking, but then broke into a jog. She'd been running with the dogs every day since Dillon had left. There had been times when she'd tired herself out to the point of exhaustion, hoping she'd be able to sleep through the night without dreaming. Once she'd dreaded sleep— now she dreaded being awake almost as much. To be awake was to have to think, and she just didn't want to think.

When they came to the woods, Christiana slowed to a walk. The dogs stayed with her, almost as though they were afraid she'd get into trouble without them. But as soon as they were out of the woods and had entered another pasture—this one belonging to Lakecroft—they couldn't run fast enough.

She raced after them, determined that this time she was going to make it all the way. And she did. All the way to the front yard, where she promptly collapsed onto the grass and lay there gasping for air.

A shadow fell over her.

Christiana raised her hand to shield her eyes from the sun and saw Dillon gazing down at her.

The look on her face must have said more than she intended, because Dillon's expression grew remarkably tender. "Hello, Christiana," he said in his deep, quiet voice.

Her eyes moved over his face feature by feature. She honestly hadn't realized until that moment just how much she'd missed him. "Hello." She tried to sound efficient as she held out her hand and let Dillon help her to her feet. "I thought you weren't coming back until tomorrow."

"I decided that I should be here when you meet Katy for the first time. She has to know she can trust you."

Neither of them noticed that Dillon was still holding her hand.

"Thank you. I . . ."

"She's here!" Stella yelled, as she ran out the door and around the house to the crushed stone driveway.

Christiana took a deep breath and looked at Dillon. "Wish me luck."

He just smiled at her. "Come on." The two of them walked around the house together. A silver Mercedes was parked next to Christiana's little sports car. An attractive woman in her sixties stepped out and smiled at Dillon. He hugged her and said something that made her smile grow even more, then he reached into the back seat to unstrap Katy from her car seat. He said something to the man in the driver's seat. Christiana stood quietly about ten feet away, waiting for her first glimpse of her niece.

Her heart caught in her throat as Dillon lifted the little girl out of the car and swung her high in his arms. She had curly red hair and clear, white skin. Her eyes were the same smoky blue as Christiana's. She was obviously delighted to see her father and wrapped her little arms around his neck, giggling infectiously.

"Oh, baby, come to Stella," the housekeeper said as she held out her arms.

Katy went happily into them.

Dillon looked at Christiana, who was standing slightly apart from the group, and was surprised to see that there were tears in her eyes. He walked over to her and tenderly touched her cheek. "What's wrong?"

She shook her head, wishing desperately she could explain it to him.

With his arm protectively around her shoulders, he walked her to where Stella was holding Katy. "Katy," he said, "This is Christiana. She's going to be living here with us and taking care of you."

Katy smiled shyly, showing two distinct dimples, and buried her face in Stella's shoulder.

"It'll take her a little while to get used to you," Dillon said. "She's gone through a lot of changes in the past couple of months."

"I understand."

Dillon kept his arm around her. It was as though he sensed she needed that contact with him at that moment. He turned her toward his parents. "Mom, Dad, this is Christiana Stevenson. She's going to be Katy's new nanny. Christiana, these are my parents, Frank and Clare Austin."

She shook each of their hands in turn, struck by the friendly warmth they exuded.

"Can you stay for a while?" Dillon asked them. "Stella's been baking this morning."

"I'm afraid not, dear," Clare Austin said with an apologetic smile. "Your father and I arranged to meet with some friends for lunch on our way home." Her eyes went to Katy and rested warmly on her curly head. "We had the most wonderful time this week. I think Katy enjoyed herself, too." Her gaze returned to her son. "Would it be all right with you if she stayed with us again in a few weeks?"

"She's a handful. Are you sure you want to do that to yourselves again?" he asked with a smile.

His mother nodded. "She's been a lifesaver for your father and me. These past two months since

Anne died would have been impossible to get through without her."

Dillon put his arms around his mother and held her for a moment, then kissed the top of her head. "Of course Katy can stay with you again. Would you like me to bring her?"

"Oh, no. We'll come for her. The drive is lovely this time of year."

Dillon's father went to the trunk and lifted out a suitcase. "Everything is clean," he told Stella as he set it on the ground. "Clare did the laundry this morning."

Katy struggled out of Stella's arms when she spotted Finn and Ian and hit the ground running. The two dogs, their fur only a few shades darker than Katy's hair, stood in front of her, their tails wagging, obviously happy to see her. Finn bumped her with his head in an attempt to get her to pet him. That was enough to knock Katy off balance and onto her rear end. She giggled delightedly and the dogs' tails wagged harder.

Mrs. Austin laughed. "I could watch her for hours." Touching Christiana's hand, she said, "Take good care of her."

"I will," she promised, wanting to reassure the nice woman.

"It was good meeting you, dear." She turned to her son and kissed his cheek. "We'll see you in a few weeks. Try not to work too hard."

Dillon opened the car door for her and helped her inside. Frank Austin, a quiet man, charmed Christiana when he smiled shyly at her, and she caught a distinct twinkle in his eyes. He hadn't said a single word to her beyond "nice to meet you," but she liked him enormously.

"Come here, Katy," Dillon called to his daughter.

She ran over to him and was scooped up into his arms. "Wave goodbye," he said, as the car pulled out.

Katy clenched and unclenched her hand in her version of a wave, aiming it at herself, rather than at her grandparents. Dillon laughed and kissed her chubby cheek.

Christiana stood watching the two of them and felt an ache in her heart. She didn't need to see any more to know that Dillon loved his daughter.

He lowered his eyes to Christiana's and met her look. "You're so serious."

"Am I?" she asked in surprise. "I'm sorry. I didn't mean to be."

A corner of his mouth lifted. "I'd love to know what you're thinking."

She pulled her eyes away. "Even I don't want to know what I'm thinking."

He looked at her curiously but didn't pursue it. "I thought that perhaps the three of us should do something together today to give you and Katy a chance to get used to each other. Any suggestions?"

Christiana thought for a moment. "A picnic?"

"That's a good idea. It's a beautiful day and we aren't going to have many more."

"And we could ride those old bikes in the barn."

Dillon nodded thoughtfully. "Sure, we could do that. I'll have to check the tires, but I know where there's an air pump. Stella!" he called to the housekeeper as she headed for the house.

"I know. I heard. It'll be ready in half an hour."

Katy struggled out of her father's arms and ran after Stella. Dillon watched until she was safely in the house, then turned to Christiana. "Come on and help me with the bikes."

"Okay."

With his hand under her arm, and Christiana very aware of it, Dillon walked her around the house to the barn she'd wandered through the day before. "These belonged to my grandparents," he said as he took the old bikes down from their pegs. "I've always liked them better than the newer ones."

"I'm surprised that the people who lived here before didn't take everything with them."

"I bought Lakecroft with all of its contents, including those in the barn," he replied.

The tires were low, so Dillon found the air pump he'd mentioned and inflated each one. While he did that, Christiana went to the unfinished rocking chair. "Is this your work?" she asked.

Dillon looked up to see what she was talking about. "Yes."

"It's beautiful."

"It will be when it's finished."

"Where did you learn to do work like this? There's such wonderful detail."

"My grandfather built a lot of the furniture that's in the house. He told me once that there was nothing in life that gave him more pleasure than building something with his own hands." Dillon gazed around the barn, a sad smile touching his mouth. "I used to spend hours in here with him, watching, and helping when he'd let me. Eventually he let me start building small, uncomplicated pieces. I think the first thing I ever made was a pencil box. I was so proud of that box. So was he."

Christiana listened quietly. "He sounds like a wonderful man."

"He was. I still miss him. Especially when I'm out here working."

Dillon checked each of the tires a final time, then stood up. "Let's get these bikes to the house. Knowing Stella, lunch is probably ready by now. And bring a jacket. The weather's unpredictable."

Dillon and Christiana walked side by side up the hill and leaned the bikes against the veranda. While Dillon got Katy and the lunch, Christiana went to her room and carelessly grabbed her jacket. The packet of letters fell to the floor. She stood looking at them for several seconds before picking them up and placing them in a drawer. "Not today, Paige. Not today," she said quietly.

She ran out of her room and got halfway down the steps, then ran back up again and got her camera case.

By the time she arrived on the veranda, Dillon had already settled Katy into a backpack-type child carrier that he'd strapped over his shoulders. A wicker picnic basket sat in the wire basket on the front of his bike.

THE JOKER GOES WILD!

Play
this
card
right!
See
inside!

IT'S A WILD, WILD, WONDERFUL
FREE OFFER!
HERE'S WHAT YOU GET:

1. *Four New Silhouette Romance™ Novels—FREE!*
   Everything comes up hearts and diamonds with four exciting romances—
   yours FREE from Silhouette Reader Service™. Each of these brand-new
   novels brings you the passion and tenderness of today's greatest love
   stories.

2. *A Lovely and Elegant Gold-Plated Chain—FREE!*
   You'll love your elegant 20k gold electroplated chain! The necklace is
   finely crafted with 160 double-soldered links and is electroplate finished
   in genuine 20k gold. And it's yours free as added thanks for giving our
   Reader Service a try!

3. *An Exciting Mystery Bonus—FREE!*
   You'll go wild over this surprise gift. It is attractive as well as practical.

4. *Free Home Delivery!*
   Join Silhouette Reader Service™ and enjoy the convenience of previewing
   six new books every month, delivered to your home. Each book is yours
   for $2.25*. And there is no extra charge for postage and handling! If
   you're not fully satisfied, you can cancel at any time, just by sending us a
   note or a shipping statement marked "cancel" or by returning any
   shipment to us at our cost.

5. *Free Newsletter!*
   It makes you feel like a partner to the world's most popular
   authors...tells about their upcoming books...even gives you their
   recipes!

6. *More Mystery Gifts Throughout the Year! No joke!*
   Because home subscribers are our most valued readers, we'll be sending
   you additional free gifts from time to time with your monthly shipments—
   as a token of our appreciation!

GO WILD
WITH SILHOUETTE® TODAY—
JUST COMPLETE, DETACH AND
MAIL YOUR FREE-OFFER CARD!

GET YOUR GIFTS FROM SILHOUETTE®
ABSOLUTELY FREE!

Mail this card today!

PLACE
JOKER
STICKER
HERE

PLAY THIS CARD RIGHT!

YES! Please send me my 4 Silhouette Romance™ novels FREE along with my free Gold-Plated Chain and free mystery gift. I wish to receive all the benefits of the Silhouette Reader Service™ as explained on the opposite page.

(U-SIL-R-11/90) 215 CIS HAYW

NAME _____
(PLEASE PRINT)

ADDRESS _____ APT. _____

CITY _____

STATE _____ ZIP CODE _____

Offer limited to one per household and not valid to current Silhouette Romance subscribers. All orders subject to approval.

SILHOUETTE READER SERVICE "NO RISK" GUARANTEE

- There's no obligation to buy—and the free books remain yours to keep.
- You don't pay for postage and handling and receive books before they appear in stores.
- You may end your subscription anytime—just write and let us know or return any shipment to us at our cost.

IT'S NO JOKE!

MAIL THE POSTPAID CARD AND GET FREE GIFTS AND $9.00 WORTH OF SILHOUETTE NOVELS—FREE!

If offer card is missing, write to:
Silhouette Reader Service, P.O. Box 1867, Buffalo, NY 14269-1867

"There you are," he said with a warm smile that set her heart pounding. "We're all ready."

Christiana looked at Katy and smiled as she put the strap of her camera bag over her head and arranged it so that it criss-crossed between her breasts. Katy smiled back. It was difficult not to just grab her and hug her, but she knew better. Katy would come to her when she was ready.

"There's a trail around the lake," Dillon said as he straddled his bike. "I think you'll enjoy it."

They rode beside one another part of the way, with Finn and Ian racing ahead as though they knew exactly where they were going. But when the trail forked and narrowed and took them away from the lake, Christiana followed behind for a mile or so.

They rode through a meadow where the foot-high grass mixed with wild wheat, appearing more gold than green as it rolled like waves in the breeze. Then they went through an apple orchard with trees that were bare and waiting for winter.

"You should see this in the spring when the trees are full of blossoms," Dillon called over his shoulder.

Christiana was so caught up in the scenery that she'd fallen behind, so she pedaled a little faster to catch up. Enchanted wasn't a strong enough word for what she was feeling. One vista was more spectacular than the next. Like the bikes they were riding, she felt as though she'd stepped back fifty years in time. And that was fine with her.

They crossed a wide stream using an old wooden footbridge like the one near Lakecroft and caught the path again as it curved through another meadow. "There's the lighthouse just ahead," Dillon said, pointing.

It was small, white and well tended, as everything on the island seemed to be. It sat on an inlet just past the meadow, about twenty yards from the ocean.

Christiana had driven along an ocean road to get to Dillon's house, but even so, she hadn't realized how near it was. In all of her ramblings during the past week, she hadn't made it this far.

They stopped just past the lighthouse. Christiana took charge of the picnic basket while Dillon lifted Katy from his back and set her on the ground. She raced off instantly to play in the sand. Dillon chased after her.

Setting the basket on the sand, Christiana opened it and spread out the blanket that Stella had packed. Kneeling on that, she started to remove the plates and food, but stopped after a moment to watch Dillon and Katy. She was screaming with laughter as her father chased her, sometimes catching her and swinging her high in the air, and sometimes letting her get away. It made Christiana smile just to watch the two of them.

Unable to resist, she reached for her camera and started taking pictures.

A freighter that was nothing more than a distant speck on the horizon caught Dillon's attention. While Katy sat on the sand and pushed the grains into tiny piles, Dillon grew still, his eyes on that speck. Christiana watched him through her camera for a long time before taking the picture. He suddenly seemed so sad. Was he thinking of his sister?

Lowering the camera to her lap, she just watched him, wanting nothing more than to put her arms around him and hold him until the hurt went away.

Katy walked over to him and stood leaning against him with one arm wrapped around his long leg. Dillon turned his head and said something to her. Katy looked up. Christiana raised her camera and took that picture.

He lifted Katy onto his shoulders and started walking toward Christiana. "Are you ready for us?" he called across the sand.

"Almost!" She put her camera on the blanket and quickly finished unpacking the peanut butter and jelly sandwiches, cold chicken and ham, some of Stella's wonderful freshly baked bread, a delicious-looking pasta salad, grape juice and lemonade.

Dillon set Katy on the blanket and sat down next to Christiana, leaning back on one elbow, his legs stretched out in front of him.

"What would you like, Katy?" Christiana asked, smiling at the little girl.

She pointed at one of the peanut butter sandwiches.

Christiana put it on a plate and cut it into quarters. "And grape juice?" she guessed.

"Grape juice," Katy repeated as accurately as she could.

Dillon took one of the big cloth napkins and tied it around Katy like a bib. "You haven't seen anything until you've seen Katy eat a peanut butter and jelly sandwich," he said smiling at Christiana.

Her heart caught and her breathing constricted. He could do that to her with a smile. "What would you like?" she managed to ask him, without giving away any of her inner turmoil.

"Chicken and a little of the salad."

She fixed his plate and one for herself.

Katy picked up part of her sandwich and started walking around. "You're very quiet," Dillon said as he watched her profile.

"This is a quiet place."

Finn and Ian came racing across the beach toward them.

"You spoke too soon," Dillon said with a laugh.

The dogs apparently had their own agenda for this picnic. Katy ran after them, waving her sandwich in the air, but the dogs, seeming to sense that she shouldn't wander too far, herded her back toward Dillon and Christiana.

"I'm impressed with the way you've handled Katy so far," Dillon said.

Christiana looked at him in surprise. "I haven't handled her at all."

"That's what I mean. You're not pushing yourself at her."

Christiana took a bite of chicken. "May I ask you a personal question?"

"That depends."

She hesitated, then plunged ahead. "Do you think Katy misses her mother?"

Dillon didn't say anything for a moment, then slowly shook his head. "I don't think so. Paige and I paid so little attention to Katy that I don't think she'd have noticed if we'd both dropped off the edge of the earth."

"You're obviously close to her now."

"She needs me," he said simply. "And I've come to love her very much."

Christiana was still trying to understand her sister. "How could a mother have a baby and then simply leave her behind as though she didn't exist?" She didn't realize she'd spoken aloud until Dillon answered.

"That depends on why one has a child to begin with. With Paige, once Katy was born and things didn't work out the way she'd planned, Katy no longer interested her."

"What things didn't work out the way she planned? I don't understand what you're saying."

Dillon watched as Katy crossed the sand toward them. "It's just as well," he said quietly. "It's an ugly little story, best left to an untold history."

"Best for whom?"

He looked at Christiana. "Everyone concerned."

Katy took another square of her sandwich and wandered off again with the dogs in tow.

Christiana took a deep breath and slowly exhaled. Her appetite had disappeared. "May I ask you another personal question?"

"Go ahead."

"Did you ever love your wife?

Dillon turned his head and looked Christiana straight in the eye. "No."

Christiana lowered her eyes. She didn't know why he'd married Paige, and she wasn't going to ask, but in that moment her heart ached for her sister. She swallowed hard to push her feelings deep down inside and turned her attention to Katy. "Leslie told me this morning that Finn and Ian were wonderful baby-sitters."

Dillon was still watching Christiana. "The three of them took to each other as soon as they met," Dillon said.

"I always wanted to have a dog when I was a child."

"Why didn't you?"

"We lived in the city. It wouldn't have been fair to the dog."

"You were never meant to live in a city."

"I didn't realize how true that was until I came to Lakecroft."

"Katy," Dillon yelled suddenly. "You're getting too close to the water. Come back here." He jumped to his feet. "I'll be back in a minute."

Christiana repacked the picnic basket and put her camera away. She didn't feel like taking pictures anymore.

Dillon returned with Katy on his shoulders. "Let's go for a walk on the beach."

Christiana got to her feet. "Oh, Katy," she said with a laugh. "Look at you." Taking a napkin from the basket she'd just packed, she wiped off Katy's sticky face and hands. "Is that better?" Christiana asked when she'd finished.

"Better."

The three of them headed across the beach. Grass grew out of the sand in patches. The wind had blown the sand into small dunes that dotted the beach. The little cove they were in circled around and Christiana could see several homes crowded together on what appeared to be an island itself, though after they had climbed the next small dune, she saw that it was in fact a sandy peninsula.

Dillon, his hands raised to hold Katy's, stopped at the top of the dune and looked around. "I don't know how I ever stayed away from here as long as I did."

Christiana took a deep breath of the ocean air. She didn't know how she was going to be able to leave when the time came. "You must have missed it terribly. I've been here for such a short time, but already I know that I'll carry this place in my heart for the rest of my life."

"Then maybe you shouldn't leave."

Her eyes met his. What would he say if he knew how she'd lied to him? She looked away as guilt washed over her.

Finn and Ian went zooming past, their paws kicking up the sand behind them. A man deep in his own thoughts rode a horse slowly along the beach close enough to the water so that the waves foamed around the horse's hooves.

Dillon looked at his watch. "We should be heading back. Even with the sun shining the way it is, I can feel the air getting cooler."

Christiana could, too. But far from minding the crispness, she enjoyed it.

Katy touched Christiana's hair. Christiana looked up at her, high on her father's shoulders, and smiled. The little girl held out her hand, as if to say she'd decided that Christiana was all right after all.

She felt strangely like crying. Katy was all that was left of her sister. Christiana raised her hand and Katy wrapped her own around two of Christiana's fingers. Just like any real family, the three of them made their way back to the picnic basket and bikes and headed for home.

It was late afternoon when they finally arrived at Lakecroft. Katy let Christiana take her out of her father's back carrier and promptly laid her red head on Christiana's shoulder, her thumb in her mouth.

"What should we do about dinner and a bath?" Christiana asked Dillon quietly over her head.

He lightly ruffled Katy's hair. "I think she's more tired than hungry. Just wash her face and hands and let her sleep. She can have a bath in the morning."

"All right." She started to go upstairs, but stopped and turned. Dillon was still there, watching her. "I didn't mean to just take over with Katy. Would you like to tuck her in?"

"I'll come up a little later. Right now it's important for the two of you to spend some time alone together."

Her blue eyes warmed. "Thank you. And thank you for the lovely day." She looked at Dillon a moment longer, then turned and continued on to Katy's room. "Here you go, sweetheart," she said as she laid Katy on her bed. "What a long day you've had."

Katy, still sucking her thumb, watched Christiana with trusting eyes.

"You don't talk very much, do you?" she said as she took off Katy's jacket and sweater. "My mom told me that I didn't say a word until I was three because I didn't want to make any mistakes. After that, they couldn't keep me quiet. Maybe it runs in the family."

Christiana went into the bathroom, soaked a cloth in warm soapy water, picked up another clean cloth, rinsed it, and slid a towel from the rack.

"Here we go," she said as she came back into the bedroom. "This is going to feel good." Taking Katy's thumb from her mouth, she washed, rinsed and dried her face, hands and arms. Then she slid a warm flannel nightgown over her head and tucked her in. "Would you like a story?"

Katy nodded.

Christiana crossed the room to the bookcase. There was a whole series of Raggedy Ann and Andy books from decades earlier. Old, old copies of every Dr. Seuss book ever written, and newer children's books that had been bought just for Katy. She took out one called *Good Night, Moon* and looked through it. It was perfect, with dark, sleepy colors and softly spoken words. The images were all geared toward sleep.

Turning out all the lights except the dim one next to the bed, Christiana sat beside Katy and held the book so that Katy could see the pictures. In a soft, low voice, she began to read, unaware of the man standing in the doorway watching.

Katy was asleep before the book was half-finished, but Christiana kept on reading for another few pages, then quietly closed it and watched the child. It was the first real chance she'd had to study her for any length of time. She pushed Katy's mop of red hair away from her face and smiled. "You are so beautiful," she said softly. "I love you already."

"She's going to love you, too," Dillon said as he came into the room.

Christiana self-consciously rose from the bed. "Katy was so tired she couldn't even stay awake for a story."

"All of that fresh air. But I warn you, she'll be up early in the morning, raring to go."

"Then so will I."

Dillon leaned over and kissed Katy on the forehead. "Good night, sweetheart," he said softly. As he straightened, he raised some beautifully carved rails that Christiana hadn't noticed into place, then went around to the other side and lifted some more, turning the bed into a crib.

"You made this, didn't you?" Christiana asked in wonder, as she examined it more closely.

"Yes. I like to be able to sit with her and read stories the way you did tonight, but that was impossible with a regular crib. This way I can read to her until she falls asleep and not have to disturb her by moving her from one bed to another.''

"Very clever.''

Dillon put his hand in the middle of her back as the two of them left the room. "What are you going to do now?'' he asked, as he pulled Katy's door half-shut.

"It's a little early for me to go to bed. I might read or something. What about you?''

"I played all day. Now I have to work.''

"On finishing that wonderful song you played for me, I hope.''

His eyes moved over her lovely face. "It's finished.''

"May I hear it?''

"Eventually.''

Ian bumped against Dillon to get his attention. "Go on,'' Dillon said as he patted the dog's head.

As though he understood—and Christiana was beginning to think both dogs understood everything only too well—Ian went into Katy's room and lay down on the floor at the foot of the bed.

"He stays with Katy all night,'' Dillon explained. "If she wakes up, he comes to get me.''

"Did you train him to do that?''

"No. It's something he started on his own soon after we moved here. Both Finn and Ian seem to think our entire extended family is their special responsibility.''

"They are the most amazing dogs.''

"Don't let them hear you calling them that.''

"What? Dogs?''

He nodded. "We haven't told them yet. They think they're human."

"I should think that would upset them more."

Dillon laughed. "The human condition being what it is and all of that, I'm inclined to agree with you." He looked at his watch. "I really have to get to work."

"Do you think it would be all right if I went to the lake for a little while?"

"Of course. Ian will let us know if Katy wakes. And I have an intercom in the music room so I can hear her. There's one in your room, as well. And a remote one you can take with you, if you're inclined."

"Where is it?"

He stepped back into Katy's room and picked up a thing that looked like a white walkie-talkie. "Just flip this switch up and you'll be able to hear her perfectly up to a thousand feet away. The lake isn't even half that far."

"Thank you." Her fingers brushed his as she took it. A simple contact, but one she felt to her toes.

Dillon felt it, as well. "I enjoyed spending the day with you, Christiana."

"I had a nice time, too," she said quietly, gazing up at him. "Katy is delightful."

His eyes remained on Christiana. "Yes, she is."

She grew uneasy under his scrutiny.

"What is it about me that makes you so uncomfortable?" Dillon asked curiously.

"Maybe I'm just one of those women who're uncomfortable around men in general."

He shook his head. "I don't think so. You're the kind of woman who would have a reason."

"And how do you know that?"

"How does one person know anything about another? I've watched you and that's my impression."

"Impressions can be misleading."

"That sounds strangely like a warning."

"I'm just imparting some of my own experience to you. What you do with it is entirely up to you. Excuse me," she said briskly as she stepped past him and went downstairs.

Dillon's dark gaze followed her.

Once she was outside, Christina gripped the handrail on the veranda and took a deep breath. This charade was getting more difficult by the hour.

Chapter Six

When she was sure that Dillon was gone, and the coast was clear, Christiana went to her room and washed her face and hands. Slipping the packet of letters into her pocket, she picked up the white remote that Dillon had given her and headed for her favorite tree.

Sinking onto the grass with a resigned sigh, she gathered her courage from the serenity of the lake, then started reading through the bundle, letter by letter. Paige's attacks on Dillon grew increasingly scathing, but what came through to Christiana was not at all what her sister had intended, but Paige's own diseased perspective.

Christiana might have believed her sister about Dillon's affairs, and the drinking and the lack of fatherly feeling, if she'd never looked into Dillon's eyes. But the Dillon in Paige's letters didn't exist, and Christiana seriously doubted if he'd ever existed. He was too well-grounded.

And now that both Dillon and Leslie had told her how Paige had neglected Katy, she noticed specifically that Paige's references to Katy grew increasingly rare.

More than an hour after she'd begun, Christiana opened the final letter that Paige had written. It hadn't been mailed, but had been found among her things after the accident. There was no envelope, no date and no salutation.

. . . If you think for one moment that I'm going to allow you to discard me, think again. You've tried to drive me away by ignoring me and by acting as though my feelings don't matter, but it isn't going to work. You're married to me and you're going to stay married to me. . . .

Christiana looked up. This had obviously been intended for Dillon. She felt as though she were trespassing onto private emotional property, but the words dragged her eyes back to them.

. . . As much as I once loved you is how much I now hate you. I want you to suffer as much as you've made me suffer, and you know I can do it. I have your sister's phone number in front of me. If you aren't here with me in one week, I'll call her and tell her the facts of life. Whatever happens from this point is completely up to you. . . .

Christiana raised her eyes from the letter and stared blindly at the lake. Anne's phone number? What did Dillon's sister have to do with any of this?

She looked back at the letter and reread it. The venom sent a chill through her.

And yet, there was a familiar ring to the words. It took Christiana a moment to travel back in time. Paige had been sixteen, Christiana fourteen. Paige had been storming around the bedroom they shared, picking up things from their dresser and slamming them back down. "He's mine," she said through clenched teeth.

"But if Justin likes someone else..." Christiana had said in an attempt to reason with her.

Paige had turned on Christiana with a look of such rage that she'd been frightened into silence. "Nobody dumps me. I dump them—when I'm ready."

Christiana jumped as a loud bark sounded near her ear. "Oh, Finn," she laughed, relieved to be taken away from her thoughts. "Am I ever glad to see you."

Finn settled onto the ground next to her, close against her outstretched leg. Christiana leaned back against the tree trunk and stroked his silky fur, her eyes on the setting sun that was burning the sky with bright orange. It flamed in the lake for a time, then disappeared, leaving darkness in its wake.

"I have to make a telephone call, Finn," she said quietly, "and I can't begin to tell you how much I'm dreading it."

The dog, his head still resting on his paw, looked up at her.

"I just can't do what my parents want me to."

She heard a noise on the walkie-talkie and held it to her ear to listen. Finn raised his head to listen also. It was just Katy rustling her blankets.

"Well," she said, slipping the letters back into her pocket and standing, "I suppose I should make that call. It isn't going to get any easier by putting it off."

Finn got up with her and the two of them strolled across the lawn. He followed her into the library and lay on a rug in front of the fireplace while she closed the door and sat in Dillon's chair behind the desk, her eyes on the phone.

"Just do it," she said to herself, and picked up the receiver to make the collect call. She spoke to the operator, and then waited, nervously drumming her fingers. Her mother accepted the charges.

"C.J., we've been waiting to hear from you. It's been a whole week. How is everything?"

"I got the job."

"We assumed that when we didn't hear from you. What are you finding out?"

"Things here aren't exactly the way you expected," Christiana said carefully.

"What do you mean?"

She chose her words carefully. "I mean that Dillon Austin doesn't seem to be the kind of man you thought he was."

There was silence on the other end of the line.

"Mom?"

"You really haven't been there long enough to come to any conclusions. It's impossible to find out much about anyone in such a short time."

"That's true to some extent. But I've watched him with Katy and it's obvious to me that he loves her very much."

"Did it occur to you that he's on his best behavior at the moment?"

"It did. And then I dismissed it. Dillon and Katy are very easy and natural together."

"And what about the things that Paige said in her letters? Have you read them yet?"

"I just finished them tonight."

"Then you know how the man really is."

"No, Mom," she said softly. "What I know is what Paige said in the letters."

There was a long pause at the other end of the line. "So you're saying that you don't believe her?"

Christiana leaned back in Dillon's chair and pushed her dark hair away from her face. "Mom, Paige was my sister and I loved her. But she had her faults. You and I both know that Paige and truth were more often strangers than companions."

"That's a terrible thing to say!"

"I don't mean to be terrible, and the last thing I want to do is hurt you. I'm just trying desperately to keep things in some kind of perspective. You've taken the Paige we knew and loved and turned her into a saint. She wasn't. You know it and I know it."

Her mother sighed. Christiana could hear the quiver in her voice. "He hurt her. He broke her heart."

"I know."

"Then how can you defend the man?"

"I'm not. I'm just seeing things here that you can't see from Arizona. Dillon is hurting, too."

"I'm sorry, but I can't work up any sympathy for him."

Christiana tiredly rubbed her forehead. "Do you remember when I was little and we'd have those long talks in the kitchen while you fixed dinner?"

"I remember." She could hear the reminiscent smile in her mother's voice.

"I was really angry one day when Susie Jensen told me something nasty she claimed Denise Franklin had said about me. I was going to cut Denise out of my life without even talking to her. And you said that I should keep an open mind. That there are two sides to every story."

"I did?"

"You did."

"What happened?"

"When I talked to Denise, I found out that what was said had become distorted into something by Susie that was never intended by Denise. Do you understand what I'm saying, Mom?"

The older woman sighed audibly over the phone. "It *is* a rather obvious point."

"But it needs to be made. Paige told us one version of what went on between the two of them. We need to hear Dillon's side, as well."

"I understand what you're saying, honey. I really do. But don't you see that he can say anything he wants now that Paige is dead?"

"And Paige could say anything she wanted in her letters because she knew we'd never confront Dillon."

"I concede the point. So what do we do now?"

"Get back to what's important. Not the relationship between Paige and Dillon, but the relationship between Dillon and Katy."

"There's a connection. If he mistreated Paige, he's certainly capable of mistreating Katy."

"And that's why I'm here. Not to judge him as a husband, but to see what kind of father he is and what kind of home he's providing for Katy."

"With an eye toward your father and me gaining custody of her. Don't forget that."

Christiana was silent.

"That's why you're there, C.J. I've lost my daughter. I'll be damned if I'll lose my granddaughter, too."

Christiana was still silent.

"C.J.? Say something."

"I know why I'm here," she said softly. "I just don't want you to get hurt again, Mom."

"That depends entirely on you, at this point."

"I know."

"Oh, honey, don't sound so sad. I know this has been a terrible burden to place on you, but you're the only one we could really trust."

"I know that, too."

"Katy belongs with us. Not with that man. That's the way Paige would have wanted it. We owe her at least that much."

"Katy belongs where she'll be the happiest."

"Exactly. Call again when you think you might have enough information for us to turn over to attorneys. And remember that our thoughts are with you. Don't forget how much we're counting on you."

Christiana closed her eyes. "I won't. Tell Dad hello for me." When she heard the click at the other end of the line, Christiana leaned forward and hung up the receiver. Tears strung the back of her eyes. She was caught in the middle. If her parents weren't able to get custody of Katy, it would break their hearts—and it would be her fault. But she couldn't lie about the kind of father Dillon was. The kind of man. Not even to make her parents happy.

Finn, seeming to sense that she needed some comforting, left his rug and sat beside her. For a moment he just looked at her. Then he lifted one paw and rested it on her leg.

"Oh, Finn," Christiana said as she wrapped her arms around him, then leaned over and buried her face in his fur, "I'm going to miss you when I leave here."

She stayed like that for a while with Finn, then rose with a sigh. As she left the library, Finn at her side, she was lost in thought to the oblivion of almost all else, including the man walking from the other direction, equally distracted. Dillon looked up first and caught her shoulders in his hands when she would have crashed into him.

"Hello," he said with a laugh.

"I'm sorry. I wasn't paying attention."

"At least I wasn't riding a horse this time."

Christiana smiled at him through her misery in the dim hall light and tried to push the conversation with her mother out of her mind.

"Did you know," Dillon asked as he touched the corner of her mouth with his fingertip, "that you get a delightful dimple right there when you smile?"

Her heart caught. "I didn't know that it was delightful, but I knew it was there."

He put his hands in his trouser pockets. "How was your walk by the lake?"

"Nice. Everything about Lakecroft is food for the soul."

"Then why do you look so sad, Christiana, even when you smile?"

"I wasn't aware that I did."

"Now you are." His eyes moved over her face. "You intrigue me."

"Because I'm sad even when I smile?" she asked, her eyes holding a touch of a sparkle.

"Because I think a man could know you for a lifetime and still find facets of your mind that would surprise and delight him," he said quietly.

"And perhaps some facets that aren't so delightful," she added.

"We all have our dark side."

"Even you?"

"Especially me." Dillon cupped her face in his hands and gazed at her. His eyes rested on her softly parted lips, even as his thumb traced their fullness. The muscle in his jaw tightened and relaxed. His eyes went back to hers. Then, without saying anything further, he walked past her.

Christiana leaned against the wall for support and put her hand over her pounding heart. "Oh, please," she whispered to the air, "don't let me fall in love with him."

After a minute, she straightened away from the wall and went upstairs to check on Katy. She could see her sleeping in the glow of a small night-light as she leaned over the crib. Her blanket had been kicked off, so Christiana tucked it around her and smoothed her curly hair away from her sleep-flushed face. For a long time she stared down at her.

Then, after patting Ian on the head, Christiana went to her own room and took the quilt from the foot of her bed. She returned to Katy and curled up in the chair next to her niece. She couldn't face being alone in her own bed and the possibility of that nightmare again.

Without even being aware of it, she drifted to sleep.

In the early hours of the morning, Dillon came in to check on Katy and found Christiana there. He smiled softly at her, then lifted her into his arms, quilt and all.

Christiana stirred and opened her eyes. "Dillon?"

"Um hmm."

"What are you doing?"

"I'm taking you to your own room. You can't sleep in a chair all night."

"I wasn't asleep."

A smile touched the corner of his mouth. "Right." Settling her onto the feather bed, he leaned over to pull the quilt up to her shoulders.

Her eyes never left him.

Dillon stopped what he was doing, his face inches from hers. "What is it, Christiana?"

"I was thinking about what you told me today at the beach."

"I told you a lot of things at the beach."

"About never having loved your wife."

"Ah," he acknowledged quietly.

"I was thinking that it must be a fate more cruel than death for a woman to love a man like you, and not be loved in return."

Dillon looked deeply into her eyes and saw a pain there he couldn't understand. He only knew he wanted to make it go away. Lowering his mouth to hers, he kissed her tenderly.

Christiana kept looking at him until the ache that filled her grew so intensely bittersweet that she couldn't any longer.

Dillon's lips left hers, reluctantly, it seemed to Christiana. He kissed the corners of her mouth, then raised his head so that he could look into her eyes. "What is it about you that makes me feel as though..."

"As though what?"

He shook his head as he touched her cheek with the back of his fingers. "I don't even know. Perhaps it's just that you make me feel at all." He kissed her forehead, then straightened away from her. "Good night, Christiana."

She watched him leave, and stared at the door long after he'd gone. She could still sense the pressure of his lips on hers.

"Good night, Dillon," she said softly.

He would feel so betrayed when he found out who she was. And he certainly would discover the truth eventually.

He'd never be able to forgive her. A solitary tear rolled unnoticed from the corner of her eye.

The next morning Dillon took a break from his work and stepped out onto the veranda. Christiana was sitting cross-legged on the grass and Katy was on her lap. Christiana pointed at the sky toward a cloud and said something. Katy looked up, too. Then she pointed. Christiana caught the little hand in hers and kissed it.

Katy got up and wandered a few feet away to poke through some leaves, found one that she liked and brought it to Christiana. As Dillon watched, Christiana took the leaf, then put her hand around Katy's waist as they discussed it, red hair touching dark hair.

Christiana rose and lifted Katy into her arms. They walked for a moment, then he heard Christiana's clear soprano voice singing a children's song. She began moving in rhythm with the song, dancing with Katy. Katy laughed and leaned her body way over to the right and then way over to the left. Christiana laughed, too, and circled and circled, holding Katy close.

Dillon's hazel eyes followed them until they were out of sight, then he quietly and thoughtfully went back into the house.

Chapter Seven

Three weeks later, Christiana ran downstairs to answer the knock on the front door. Leslie stood on the porch, grinning at her. "Can you come out and play?"

Christiana burst out laughing.

"I haven't asked anyone that question since I was ten! And as it happens, I'm quite sincere. I know that Dillon's gone and that Katy's with her grandparents, so I left Cameron with John and came over here. Let's go for a ramble in the woods."

"I'd love to. Come on in for a minute while I get my jacket and camera."

Leslie waited in the hall while Christiana ran back upstairs. It was chilly out so she put on a thick pink jacket and draped a knit scarf around her neck. Pulling out her camera, she checked to make sure she had plenty of film, then hung the camera bag so that the straps crossed diagonally between her breasts.

"Ready," she said as she went downstairs. "I just have to tell Stella we're going."

"Going where?" Stella asked as she walked into the front hall, wiping her hands on a kitchen towel.

"Rambling," Leslie said.

"Rambling where?"

"Wherever the mood takes us," Leslie said.

"Would you like to come, Stella?" Christiana asked. "The house looks perfect and you've been cooking all morning. A little fresh air would be good for you."

Stella lifted an expressive eyebrow. "At my age, a little fresh air could kill me." She wrapped Christiana's scarf more warmly around her neck. "Mind you two don't catch a chill. Now run along and have fun."

Leslie tossed a look at Christiana as they went outside. "You've certainly won Stella over. She treats you like you're one of the family—and that's saying something."

"She's nice to everyone."

"Well, she did tell me not to catch a chill," Leslie said thoughtfully as they strolled across the lawn and headed for the pasture. "But that's probably because she's just afraid that if I get sick, she'll get stuck feeding John."

Christiana laughed again. "This is nice. I'm glad you came over, Leslie."

"Me, too. I wouldn't trade my life for anything, but there are times when I need to get away, even if it's just for a few hours. Let's take the footbridge across the stream.''

Christiana stopped halfway across and raised the camera to her eye. Click. Then she sat on the bridge and focused through the wood rails. Click.

"How did you get interested in photography?" Leslie asked, as she sat down next to her.

"A relative gave me a camera when I was six and I've been taking pictures ever since." She raised the camera to her eye again and tried turning it sideways. "I know exactly how I want this to look, but I can't get the right angle from up here." She lifted the camera bag over her head and handed it to Leslie.

"What are you doing?" Leslie asked as Christiana climbed over the railing.

"I want to get closer to the water so that I can get the tunnel effect of the trees."

"But . . ."

Christiana lowered herself over the side of the bridge and stepped onto one of the crossboards attached to a wood piling. Bracing herself, she raised the camera and focused. That was exactly what she was looking for. Click. She took a second one for good measure.

Leslie leaned over the bridge. "You're crazy."

"I know." She handed her the camera and climbed back up. "But I got a great shot."

They crossed over the bridge and took a path into the woods, their steps hushed by the carpet of damp leaves.

"I think it's going to snow tonight," Leslie said, her breath steaming in the crisp air. "And I can't even bring myself to complain about it. We've had such an unusually mild fall."

Christiana stopped walking and looked around, her face alight with pleasure. "It's so beautiful here. Do you ever take this place for granted?"

"Sometimes, sure. But then I'll see a sunset that brings me up short, or I'll watch some geese flying overhead. Or I'll simply open my eyes and look."

"Did you ever think about leaving the island?"

"Not really. At least not seriously. This is my home. It's John's home. My family has been here for generations." She looped her arm through Christiana's as they walked. "What about you? Do you miss the city?"

Christiana took a deep breath of the fresh air. "Not a bit. I think I'd be quite content to spend the rest of my life here."

"Then do it."

"I'm afraid that's not an option."

"Why not?"

"I wish I could talk to you about it, Leslie. It would be an incredible relief, but I can't."

"Not now or not ever?"

"Not now. I don't know about ever."

"That sounds ominous."

Christiana looked at her and smiled as she thought about how fond of Leslie she'd grown. Always in the back of her mind when they were together was the fact that Leslie was going to find out the truth about her one day, and then what would happen to their friendship? But thinking about that wasn't going to make it go away.

"Let's not talk about dreary things today. Let's just enjoy ourselves."

"I can do that." She leaned against a tree and tilted her face toward the sun. "How's this for a pose?" she asked, fluffing her hair.

"Completely natural." Christiana said dryly, as she focused and snapped a picture.

"Do you think I could have a copy of that?"

They fell into step with each other. "Of course. But I think we'll have a better one before the day's over."

"And I know right where I want it taken. Come on." They walked and walked. Christiana knew they were getting closer to the ocean because the texture of the air changed and the wind picked up.

And then they were there, standing on a cliff that overlooked the ocean while the wind whipped at them.

"What do you think?" Leslie asked.

"I'm not thinking at all," she said softly. "I'm just drinking it in."

The sky had grown increasingly dark while they'd been walking, but here the sun shot through the clouds in scattered beams aimed at the rough water. Waves smashed into the base of the cliff some forty feet below them and sent a salt spray into the air.

Leslie looked at the sky and shook her head. "I really think we should be heading back. Those are definitely snow clouds."

"Just a few more minutes." Christiana changed camera lenses and added a pinkish filter, then began shooting. When Leslie was least expecting it, Christiana aimed at her and snapped what her instincts told her was going to be a remarkable portrait.

Leslie looked at her with narrowed eyes. "That was sneaky. I wasn't ready."

"Yes you were. You'll see."

"Humph." She suddenly grew very still, her face raised to the sky. "I felt something."

Christiana raised her face as well. "Me, too."

"Snow."

"Not much, though."

"It's still early. There's going to be a lot more before this is finished. My house is closest. We'll go there and then John can take you home."

The two of them began walking briskly as the snow started to fall a little more heavily. Christiana kept pace as she packed everything into the camera bag and fastened it.

"Do you mind if I ask you a personal question?" Leslie asked.

Christiana looked at her in surprise. "You ask me personal questions all the time but that's the first time you've ever asked permission."

"Even I have my tactful moments. Do you mind?"

"Of course not."

"How do you feel about Dillon?"

"I think he's a very nice man," she answered safely.

"I didn't ask what you think about him. I asked how you feel."

"I don't know how I feel."

"There you go again," Leslie said in exasperation. "Whenever we talk about Dillon, you get evasive."

"Since when is not knowing something considered being evasive?"

Leslie looked at Christiana from the corner of her eyes. "I'm sorry. I'm being pushy again."

"Yes, you are."

"I'll stop."

Christiana looked at her skeptically.

"In a minute. Look, I've been watching the two of you these past weeks. Something is going on between you."

"You're wrong."

"I'm never wrong about these things. I've known Dillon for years and I've never seen him look at another woman the way he looks at you."

"It's not love, believe me. He's trying to figure out what makes Christiana tick."

"And I've seen the way you look at him."

"He's an attractive man. Of course I look at him."

"But that's all there is to it?"

That's all she'd allow it to be, Christiana thought.

"Does your reluctance about Dillon have anything to do with his first marriage?"

"I thought you only wanted to ask one question."

"I take it this is the end of the conversation?"

"This particular one, yes."

"Are you annoyed with me?"

Christiana laughed and shook her head. It wouldn't do any good to get annoyed. "You're really something."

"All right. Just one more remark and then I'll stop. You and Dillon need to open up your eyes and see what's standing right in front of you. End of lecture."

Christiana grew quiet. The woman Dillon would see wouldn't be the one he thought he was seeing. Any kind of trust she'd managed to build with him during her time here would be—was going to be—destroyed. Sometimes she just wanted to run away and not have to face any of this.

"It's getting colder," Leslie said.

Christiana looked around.

The snow was coming down a little harder and was beginning to cover the ground. She wrapped her scarf more snugly around her neck and gazed around with a photographic artist's eye. "Leslie, look at how the snow is starting to stick to one side of the trees. I bet it's going to be beautiful in the moonlight."

"I'd enjoy it more if the snow weren't starting to stick to me, as well. Besides, there isn't going to be any moonlight tonight. Too many clouds."

The wind suddenly changed direction and blew a gust of snow straight into their faces. Leslie let out an offended squeal. "Remember what I said earlier about not complaining about the winter because we'd had such a long fall?"

"Um hmm."

"I lied. I'm not ready for winter yet. I'm never ready for winter when it arrives."

"It's not that cold, Leslie. I don't think it's much below freezing."

"And how much below freezing does the temperature have to go before you consider it cold?"

Christiana looked at her friend and laughed. "You certainly got testy all of a sudden."

"Stop trying to cheer me up. I don't want to cheer up. It's always been my custom to start complaining about the weather when the first snowflake hits the ground and to keep it up on and off until spring comes. Everyone expects it of me."

"I promise not to cheer you up if you promise not to depress me. I want to enjoy my first snow on Prince Edward Island."

"Oh, all right. I'll try."

"Thank you."

"But for the second snow all bets are off."

"That goes without saying."

"We're almost home, anyway. How much damage can I do to your psyche in fifteen minutes?"

"I wouldn't want to put it to the test."

Leslie opened a pasture gate and then refastened it as soon as they'd passed through. It was getting dark in earnest now, and Christiana could see the welcoming lighted windows of Leslie's house in the distance. A little curl of smoke rose from one of the chimneys. Christiana stopped walking and took out her camera.

Leslie had continued walking until she suddenly noticed she was alone. "What are you doing?" she asked in disbelief when she turned back, only to find Christiana changing camera lenses again.

"I want to take a picture of your house just the way it is right now."

"Oh, for heaven's . . ."

"It reminds me of that painting by Maxfield Parrish called *Hilltop Farm*. Have you ever seen it?" She raised the camera to her eye and adjusted the settings.

"I don't know. I may have."

The shutter clicked, but Christiana kept the camera raised to her eye.

Leslie suddenly put her face right in front of the lens. "I'm cold. I'd like to go home now."

"Right," Christiana said sheepishly as she put her camera back in the bag. "Sorry."

"Remind me not to be walking with you if there's ever some kind of impending natural disaster."

"You'll thank me when it's developed."

They were nearly to the house when Christiana stopped and put a hand on Leslie's arm. "I think I'd like to walk to Lakecroft rather than have John take me."

"But it's thirty minutes away."

"I don't mind. In fact, I'm enjoying myself."

"In a few minutes it's going to be completely dark. You'll get lost."

"All I have to do is walk in a straight line through two pastures and a woods. I think I can handle it."

The wind whipped the snow between them. "Aren't you cold?" Leslie asked, as she wrapped her arms around herself.

"A little, but I don't mind. I have some thinking I need to do and this is the perfect time."

Leslie shook her head. "All right. I give up. Go ahead and walk, but call me the minute you get home."

"I will."

"And don't forget because I'm going to be a nervous wreck until I hear from you. Warm, but a nervous wreck nonetheless."

"I promise." She kissed Leslie on the cheek. "Thanks for a wonderful afternoon. I really enjoyed it."

Leslie stood there for a moment and watched Christiana's disappearing back. She wasn't going to wait for Christiana to call her. She was going to call Lakecroft straightaway. Maybe Dillon was back. He could watch for her.

Christiana was about ten minutes into her walk when she realized she'd made a big mistake. The snowfall had gone from light to moderate to a blizzard in minutes, blanketing everything it touched, including her. An icy blast of wind hit her full in the face, sending stinging snow onto her cheeks.

Turning her back on the wind, she took the scarf from around her neck and wrapped it around her head and face, then jammed her hands into her pockets to keep them warm.

Relief flooded through her when she finally made it to the woods because then she knew she was nearly halfway home.

But the woods seemed strangely unending. Visibility was down to almost nothing. She could barely make out her hand in front of her face, but she could have sworn she'd been walking in a straight line.

Half an hour later, Christiana knew she was in trouble. She couldn't find her way out. And she was really cold. The warmth from her body had melted the snow on her jeans. They were soaked and so was she.

She finally stopped walking altogether, afraid she was only making things worse, and tried desperately not to panic. By this time, she told herself, Leslie had called Lakecroft to find out why Christiana hadn't called her. John was probably out looking for her right at that moment. She'd just find a little haven and calmly wait to be rescued.

Her haven turned out to be a small clump of trees that had grown in a semicircle. She crouched in the center and buried her face in her arms to protect as much of herself from the wind as she could manage.

How long she sat like that, Christiana didn't know. It seemed like forever, but in reality was probably no more than an hour.

Finn found her first. Christiana didn't even know he was there until he barked next to her ear.

Laughing with relief, Christiana wrapped her arms around the snow-covered dog and hugged him. "Am I ever glad to see you!"

He happily licked her a few times and then ran off before she had a chance to follow him. "Finn!" she called as she rose and narrowed her eyes against the sheet of snow that was falling. "Come back!"

She heard him bark. It sounded far away.

Her heart sank.

"Christiana!"

She paused before she answered because it wasn't the voice she was expecting.

"Christiana!"

"Dillon? Dillon? I'm over here!"

"Keep yelling so I can find you!"

"I'm over here! Over here!" Even though she knew he couldn't see her, she waved wildly.

Finn came back; then left and came back again. That was when she realized that he was, in his way, leading Dillon to her. And it worked. She saw a light clouded by snow coming closer and she ran toward it, stopping within inches of Dillon's horse. "I'm so glad you're here," she gasped, her scarf and camera bag trailing on the ground behind her. "I don't think I've ever been so glad to see anyone in my entire life."

Dillon jumped off the horse and took her by the shoulders. "Are you all right?"

"I'm fine. Just lost and cold."

"You are the most ... I should have just ... I've never met a woman who can get herself into so much trouble. It would have served you right if I'd just left you out here for the night." And with that he pulled her into his arms and kissed her.

Christiana's body tensed, but all resistance faded as her body began to slowly fill with Dillon's warmth. She raised her arms and tangled her fingers in his snow-wet hair as the kiss deepened and took over her senses.

Dillon raised his head and looked into her eyes in the dull light coming from the lamp attached to the horse's saddle. "You have to take better care of yourself. I don't know what I'd do if anything happened to you."

He pulled her more tightly into his arms and just held her. "Oh, Christiana," he said against her ear, his voice full of quiet resignation. "Come on. I'll take you home."

With his hands at her waist, he lifted her onto the saddle, then picked up the camera bag she'd unknowingly dropped to the ground before climbing up behind her.

"What were you thinking, to walk home in weather like this?" Dillon asked as he wrapped his arms around her and pulled her back against his chest.

"I wanted some time to be alone so I could think. And it wasn't like this when I started walking."

Dillon kneed the horse, and with Finn trotting beside them, they made their way out of the woods.

The snow was still blinding. Even with the light, Christiana could see little or nothing. "How can you tell where we are?" she asked.

"Years of practice."

Christiana turned her head sideways and looked up at him. Dillon looked at her at the same time, and kissed the tip of her cold nose. "We'll be home in about ten minutes. A hot bath and some tea and you'll be as good as new."

That wasn't it. She could handle being wet and cold.

What she couldn't handle was the revelation that had struck her the minute she'd heard Dillon's voice calling to her. A revelation she'd been avoiding almost since the day she'd arrived here. She'd fallen in love with her dead sister's husband.

They were almost on top of the house before Christiana could see the light in the windows.

"You go on in. Get out of those wet clothes and into a hot bath," Dillon said. "I have to dry the horse and stable him."

Christiana slid to the ground without looking at Dillon, then went inside and climbed the stairs to her room. Stella had lit the fireplace before leaving for the day, but it had died down. Christiana tossed two logs on it and stood watching while the flames found their way around them.

Going to her bathroom, she peeled off her wet clothes and dropped them onto the tile with a splat. Then she stepped into the shower and stood still, her eyes closed as the warm water cascaded over her cold body. She stayed there for perhaps fifteen minutes, unmoving.

But she couldn't stay there forever, so she got out, dried herself and put on the warm cotton nightgown that hung on the back of the door. Her hair was still damp, even after being toweled off, but she knew the fire would take care of that. Turning off the light in her room, she wrapped herself in the quilt and sat on the floor in front of the fireplace.

There was a knock.

Christiana stared at the door for a long time before saying anything. "Come in, Dillon."

As he stood in the doorway with the light of the hall behind him, she could see that he'd changed into dry clothes and was holding a cup of tea. "I thought maybe you'd be in bed by now," he said as he crossed the room and handed it to her.

"No. I'm just enjoying the fire."

He sat next to her with a tired sigh. "I called Leslie to tell her that you'd been rescued."

"Thank you."

He nodded and stared into the flames.

Christiana studied his profile. She could have looked at him forever. "I wasn't expecting you back tonight."

"I didn't expect to come back tonight, but the feeling that you needed help kept nagging at me."

"I know you're not going to believe this, but I'm usually a very competent person. It's just since coming here that I seem to get into so much trouble."

"I'm not complaining," he said quietly as he looked at her in the firelight. "I think it's rather charming." Dillon abruptly stood up, leaned over and kissed the top of her head. "Good night, Christiana."

She watched him leave, her heart in her eyes.

The door closed quietly behind him.

Christiana pulled her legs up to her chest and wrapped her arms around them as she stared into the fire. No one was going to be able to rescue her from this mess.

Dillon stood outside her door, his hand still on the knob. Then it slowly dropped to his side and he walked away.

Chapter Eight

Christiana sat straight up in bed, her heart hammering in a horribly familiar way. Her terrified screams still echoed around the dark room.

Dillon came running in, wearing just his drawstring pajama bottoms, and pulled her into his arms without asking any questions. He held her tightly, rocking her back and forth and smoothing her hair until she was calm.

"Thank you," she said as she leaned back and away from him, desperately trying not to meet his eyes. "It was just a bad dream. I'm all right now."

"No, you're not, Christiana." Dillon raised her face to his. "Tell me what it is that makes you scream in the night. Maybe I can help. At least let me try."

She shook her head, but now that she was looking

at him, she couldn't look away. "I can't. Would you just hold me for a little while?"

Dillon climbed into bed beside her, then gently pulled her down with him so that her cheek was pillowed by his solid chest. He kissed the top of her silky head as he covered them both with the blanket and wrapped her in his arms. "Better?"

She nodded and took a shaky breath.

Dillon held her closer.

Christiana tried to push the nightmare out of her mind and let Dillon fill her senses.

Dillon. His skin smelled clean. Not fragranced, but clean, as though he'd just showered. Her arm rested lightly across his flat stomach, her hand higher on his chest. She could feel the texture of his skin through her fingertips.

As they lay there in the stillness of the room, Christiana held her breath and listened. "I can hear your heart beating," she whispered.

He rubbed his rough cheek against her hair. "And I can feel yours."

She raised her head so that she was lying on the pillow facing him.

Dillon looked into her eyes as he touched her cheek with a gentle hand. "Don't look at me that way." His gaze moved over her face. "My resistance to you isn't at its strongest right now."

"We need to talk."

"I know. And we will. But not tonight."

She lowered her cheek to his chest again.

Dillon held her closer. "Go to sleep."

They lay in silence.

"Dillon?" she said softly.

"Umm?"

I love you. The words were there. The feelings were there. And so was everything between them. But she couldn't say it. "Nothing. Good night."

Dillon's hand stroked her arm.

Again they lay quietly for a time.

Then Christiana raised her head again and looked at Dillon. "Are you ever going to let Katy meet her maternal grandparents?"

He looked at her in surprise. "Where did that question come from?"

"It's something that's been bothering me and I want to know. Are you going to let her spend time with them?"

"No," he said tersely.

"Why not?"

"As far as I'm concerned, that part of Katy's heritage doesn't exist."

"They might be nice."

"We're talking about the same people who raised Paige. I don't want them near my daughter."

She rubbed her cheek against his shoulder and sighed. Somewhere along the line, he was going to have to compromise. There had to be some kind of middle ground she could find between Dillon and her parents.

But she couldn't think about that any more tonight. She couldn't think about anything. She was emotionally exhausted. If she could have had one wish, it would have been that she could wake tomorrow and find her sister alive and herself anywhere but in the arms of a man she'd been deceiving since the day they'd met.

Christiana closed her eyes. Dillon's chest evenly rose and fell beneath her cheek. She was so aware of her body pressed against the hard length of his.

At that moment, the way she felt about Dillon overwhelmed her. It filled her to the exclusion of anything else.

And despite the knowledge of how this all must end for her in the days ahead, for now, in the arms of the man she loved, Christiana felt warm and safe. For the first time in a long time, she wasn't afraid to sleep.

Christiana woke slowly the next morning. She buried her face in her pillow and smiled. It smelled of Dillon.

Dillon. She quickly opened her eyes and looked around. He was gone.

She dressed quickly and ran downstairs. "Stella," she said breathlessly as she burst into the kitchen, "where's Dillon?"

"Oh, honey, he left more than an hour ago for Vancouver. Some business about the music he's been working on."

"When will he be back?"

"A week. Maybe two."

Christiana sank onto a chair.

"What's the matter?" Stella asked, as she sprinkled some flour into a big bowl.

"I wanted to talk to him."

"Sounds important."

"It is. Very."

"I have a phone number you could call."

"No. Thanks anyway. What I have to say to him can't be said over the phone." She thought for a moment and came to a decision. "I have to leave, Stella. There's some personal business I need to take care of. I'll be back long before Katy."

"Any message for Dillon?"

"No. Just tell him that I'll see him soon." She looked at her watch. "I'd better get going."

Stella picked up a dish towel and dried her hands. "I'll help you pack."

"It's all right. I have clothes where I'm going."

Christiana stared out the window as the taxi pulled into the circular drive of her parents' huge white stucco winter home. The maid, a young woman Christiana didn't know very well, answered the door.

"Hello, Constanza," she said as she walked past her into the tile foyer. "Are my parents in?"

"Yes, ma'am. I'll tell them you're here."

"Thank you. I'll be waiting in the living room."

While the maid disappeared into one of the wings, Christiana went into an enormous living room just off the foyer. It was decorated completely in white, with touches of accent colors. Her mother had always loved white. Christiana liked it, too, but in moderation.

As she stood in the room now, for the first time in a long time, she realized why she'd never really liked this house. It was too perfect. This wasn't the kind of home where you'd read the newspaper and leave it sitting on the coffee table.

"C.J.!" her mother cried as she entered the room and hugged her. "We weren't expecting you. You should have called so we could have made plans for an evening out."

"I didn't decide to come until the last minute. Hi, Dad," she said to the silver-haired man who came in behind his wife.

He gave her a warm hug. "Hello, sweetheart. Good to see you. Maybe we could get in a round of golf."

"I'm sorry, but I can't stay."

He sat on the couch and patted the cushion beside him. "What's the hurry?"

"I have to get back to the island."

"Get back?" her mother asked, as she sat across from them. "I assumed that the reason you came here is because you'd gotten what you needed from that place."

"That's what I want to talk to you about."

"I see." Her mother leaned back against the couch. "You're obviously bringing bad news."

"I guess that depends on how you look at it."

"And how do *you* look at it?"

Christiana took a deep breath and plunged in. "I think Katy is a very lucky little girl. She has a wonderful home and is surrounded by people who love her. Including her father."

"So what you're saying is that you didn't get any hard evidence that will help us get custody of the child," her mother said.

"There isn't any to get. Katy is where she belongs."

Marian Stevenson White looked at her daughter a long time before speaking. "I knew after your last phone call that that man had gotten to you. For heaven's sake, Christiana, don't let him do to you what he did to our poor Paige."

Christiana reached out and touched her mother's hand. "No one is doing anything to me. It's just that I've lived in the same house with Dillon and Katy for an entire month. He has no idea who I really am and hasn't had any reason to be on his best behavior. What I've found at Lakecroft is a warm, friendly home and a father who loves his daughter very much."

"And if you were called in to court to testify, that's what you'd say?"

"I'd have to."

Her mother's eyes filled with tears.

"Oh, Mom, please..."

Marian rose from the couch, walked to the window and stood looking outside with her back to the room. "I suppose a good lawyer could make a case for us anyway. We lead a much more stable life than that—musician." The very word seemed to leave a bad taste in her mouth. "We simply won't mention what you've found one way or another."

"You're not hearing me, Mom. Katy is happy. I don't think you should try to get custody of her."

Her mother turned. "That little baby is all we have left of Paige. I refuse to leave her with a man who thought so little of his own wife that he couldn't even be bothered to show up for her funeral."

"I don't know why he did that," she said quietly. "It's not what I would have expected of him. But that still has nothing to do with Katy."

Her mother's eyes sparked. "Then what exactly do you propose we do? Forget that we have a granddaughter?"

"No, no, nothing like that. I think you should be to Katy exactly what you are—her grandparents. She's a loving child with more than enough room in her heart for everyone. Go to Prince Edward Island and visit her, the way grandparents would. See for yourself how she lives. Meet Dillon and judge him through your own eyes, not through Paige's. But please don't try to take Katy away from her world. Believe me, she won't thank you for it. Not now, and certainly not later."

Her mother left the window and came to stand in front of Christiana. She was angry and it showed in the rigid lines of her body. "Are you in love with him?"

Christiana's heart sank. "Mom, I . . ."

"Are you in love with Dillon Austin? Answer me."

Christiana forced herself to look her mother straight in the eye. "Yes."

Her mother's expression turned into one of disgust. "What kind of woman are you? What kind of woman would take a man into her heart who did what Dillon Austin did to her own sister? Is this the way we raised you?"

The backs of Christiana's eyes burned with tears, but she didn't let them fall.

"Paige's memory deserves better than this from you. And I'll tell you something else, young lady. If you have anything further to do with Dillon Austin, your father and I will consider ourselves to have lost two daughters, not one."

"Marian!" Christiana's father rose from the couch and faced his wife. "That's an awful thing to say."

"I meant every word of it." She turned away from both of them and strode from the room.

Christiana's father put his arms around his daughter's sagging shoulders. "She didn't really, you know."

"Oh yes she did, Dad."

"I'll talk some sense into her."

"It won't change anything."

He didn't say so, but he knew that it was probably true.

Christiana walked to the window. She'd known that she couldn't have a relationship with Dillon. She'd known it even as she was falling in love with him. And not just because of her parents. There were also the lies.

"So what will you do now?"

"Go back to Lakecroft. I have to tell Dillon the truth about myself. I owe him at least that much."

"What do you think his reaction will be when he finds out you're Paige's sister?"

She shook her head. "I don't know. I just don't know. Things went on between Dillon and Paige that none of us are aware of. They must have been horrible, though."

Her father didn't say anything.

"What I hope to do is convince him to let you and Mom visit Katy."

"Do you think you can do that?"

"Dillon is a reasonable man. At the moment he has you and Mom painted with the same brush as Paige, but when he's had a chance to think things through, he'll come to the right decision. His first concern is Katy."

"Now all we have to do is convince your mother that visitation is enough."

"She'll come around. Particularly if it's the only way she's going to get to see Katy."

Christiana's father touched her shoulder. "If it helps any, I don't believe for a minute that your mother would cut you out of her life. But the kind of betrayal of Paige that your falling in love with her ex-husband would involve would break her heart. She's not strong right now. I don't know how much more she can take."

"I know." Christiana got to her feet. She didn't want to talk about this anymore. "I have to be leaving. Tell Mom goodbye for me. And tell her not to worry. I'll do the right thing."

"You always do. Can't you spend the night?"

"I think I'd rather get back to Lakecroft. I need time to gather my thoughts and gear up my courage before I talk to Dillon." She kissed her father's cheek. "I'll call as soon as I know something definite."

"C.J." Christiana was halfway to the door, but turned when her father said her name. "I love you, you know. So does your mother. She just doesn't know how to say it sometimes."

"I know. And I hope you know that I would never do anything to hurt you."

Christiana walked to a pay phone and called a taxi.

She spent that night at a hotel, and it wasn't until late the following night that she made it back to Lakecroft. The house was dark. Stella would have gone home long before, and neither Dillon nor Katy were back yet.

Even so, Christiana was glad to be there. In the short time she'd lived there, this place had become home to her. She was going to miss it terribly.

Taking the key from under a flowerpot near the door, she let herself in. No sooner had she opened the door than the phone started to ring and Finn and Ian started to bark. Running inside, she managed to get to the library without tripping over either dog, and flipped on the light just before grabbing the phone. "Hello," she said breathlessly.

There was a surprised pause at the other end of the line. "Christiana?"

Her heart moved into her throat at the sound of that deep voice. "Dillon!" She clutched the receiver with both hands. "Hello. How are you?"

"I called last night, but Stella said you'd gone."

"I had some personal matters to attend to."

"And you came back."

There was something in the tone of his voice. "Did you think I wouldn't?"

"I wasn't sure, Christiana. You've given out mixed signals ever since you arrived."

She sat on the edge of the desk. "I know I have, and I'm sorry."

"I've often thought that one of these days you'd simply disappear from my life, never to return."

"I'd never leave without telling you."

"I know Katy's been gone a lot the past few weeks and you haven't had much to do, but that will be changing soon."

"It isn't that." She paused. "Dillon, there are some things I need to talk to you about. Very important things."

"All right." He sounded as though he'd been expecting something like that. "I'll get home as quickly as I can."

"Thank you."

She hung up the phone, but stayed where she was and traced over the receiver with the tip of her forefinger. "Oh, Dillon," she whispered, "how am I going to tell you?"

Finn bumped her with his nose.

She obligingly scratched the top of his head. Ian, not about to be outdone, moved his head into position under her other hand. She scratched him, too.

They followed her upstairs and sat in her room while she showered and changed into comfortable jeans and a heavy sweater. Lifting the mystery novel she'd been reading from her bedside table, she went downstairs to the library again and looked around.

It was a wonderful room, but chilly, so she lit the fire that Stella had already laid out.

Lying on the couch in front of it, she pulled a blanket over herself and stared into the fire, watching as the paper and kindling caught and the flames began licking around the large logs. The fragrant smell of the apple wood filled the air.

Finn and Ian took up positions at opposite ends of an oval rug between the couch and the fireplace and promptly fell asleep.

Christiana turned the book slightly so that she could see the pages in the firelight and began reading. It was the only way to take her mind off tomorrow.

She didn't remember falling asleep, or the book falling to the floor from her limp hand. She didn't hear the front door open or the dogs leaving the library. And she didn't hear Dillon as he poked at the fire and put on another log, then sat by the couch to watch her sleep.

She didn't know what woke her, but when she opened her eyes, she found herself looking at Dillon.

Startled, she tried to sit up, but Dillon lightly touched her shoulder. "You look comfortable. Just stay there."

"Dillon, I wasn't expecting you tonight."

"I almost didn't make it, but a friend of mine loaned me his plane."

Her heart sank and it showed it. Neither of them heard the front door open and close or saw Stella standing just outside the library.

"What's wrong?" he asked quietly.

"I wanted to have time to prepare what I have to say to you rather than simply blurting it out."

He looked at her for a long moment. "I see. This really is serious then."

"Oh, Dillon, you've no idea."

"Whatever it is can't possibly be as horrible as you think at this moment."

"Yes, it can."

"Then simply tell me and get it over with."

She looked into his eyes, steeling herself. "Dillon, my full name is Christiana Jean Stevenson White. Paige was my sister."

Chapter Nine

Dillon looked at her blankly for a full thirty seconds, not believing what he'd heard. "What?"

"I'm Paige's sister."

Dillon got to his feet and dragged his fingers through his hair. "My God."

Christiana sat up, but stayed on the couch. Her knees were trembling so much she didn't know if they'd support her if she tried to stand.

He stared at her in the firelight. "I knew you had some sort of secret, but this..." His eyes grew hard. "And I thought you were different. I opened my home to you. I accepted you into this family. I trusted you with my daughter and all the time you were lying. For what? What possible reason could you have?"

"Katy. My parents and I were worried about her. We wanted to make sure she was being well cared for."

"Why didn't you just ask? Or send someone from some social service? Why was it necessary for you to insinuate yourself into our lives? Into my life."

Christiana didn't say anything. She couldn't bear the way he was looking at her.

"You may not look anything like Paige, but you're certainly sisters under the skin, aren't you?"

"If I'd told you who I was, you never would have hired me."

"Damn right." He threw the words at her.

"Please try to understand. This situation isn't all black and white."

"By all means, explain it to me, Christiana. Help me to see the subtle shadings of gray."

Christiana rose from the couch and paced in front of the fireplace, passing within a foot of Dillon. When she'd collected her thoughts, she stopped, facing him across the length of the oval rug. "Paige has always been the light of my parents' lives. She was beautiful and golden and challenging to raise. She was very special to them."

Dillon just looked at her.

"When she was killed, it left a terrible void in my parents' lives." She looked at him for some kind of reaction.

There was none except an anger barely held in check.

"Paige had told my parents things about you."

"Such as?"

"You neglected her and spent all of your time traveling."

"True."

"She said you didn't even see Katy until she was three months old and even then took no interest in her."

"Also true." Dillon didn't even attempt to defend himself.

"She was very unhappy and my parents blamed—and still blame—you. And they're particularly bitter that you didn't come to the funeral or in any way acknowledge her death."

"I come off as quite a scoundrel."

"That's what I thought."

"Thought?"

Her eyes locked with his. "I don't know what went on between you and Paige, but I know that the Dillon Austin I know is a decent, caring, good man."

His look didn't soften.

"Dillon, you have to understand what my parents were going through. They're good people who'd lost a daughter they dearly loved. That daughter had a child who was being raised by a man they had reason to despise. They assumed you had a certain lifestyle and they wanted me to gather enough evidence against you to use in court in a custody battle for Katy."

"And you agreed to something like that?" His voice was deep with disappointment. "You, Christiana? Why?"

Christiana looked down at her hands. "I owed them at least that. And I also wanted to make sure

that Katy was all right. The only information I had
to go on was what Paige had told me and written in
her letters to Mom and Dad. I had to see for myself."

The muscle in his jaw tightened. "So you came to
Lakecroft."

"And I found a wonderful home and a good father and a very happy little girl. That's what I went
to Arizona to tell my parents. I also told them that I
didn't think they should seek custody of Katy. I'm
hoping that you'll allow them to visit Katy and be
real grandparents to her. They're good people.
Whatever bad things happened between you and
Paige had nothing to do with my parents and they
shouldn't be punished for them."

Dillon took his eyes off Christiana for the first
time since she'd begun talking and stared into the
fire. Then he picked up the jacket he'd tossed over
the arm of a chair and put it on. "I'm going out for
a while."

"Don't hate me for what I did," she pleaded.

"I'm going out for a while," he repeated. "I'll be
back when I get back."

"Dillon..."

"I need some time alone."

"All right, but while you're out, think about this.
I didn't do anything that you wouldn't have done for
your family. I'm sorrier than I can say that I lied to
you, but I'd do it again if I was given the same
choices. Even knowing as I do now that I'd fall in
love with you and that it would end like this."

Dillon looked at her for a long time. "The irony of all this," he said quietly, "is that I fell in love with you, too." He turned and left the room.

As soon as she heard the front door close, Christiana leaned against the fireplace wall for support. She felt ill and weak and hopeless. Dillon had loved her and she'd betrayed him.

However things worked out, there was one thing she knew for certain: there would be no happy ending for her.

She made her way slowly upstairs. She hadn't realized it was morning until she looked out her window. Walking over to it, she searched for some sign of Dillon. There was none—but still she searched. After a while, she carried her luggage downstairs and put it in the front hall by the door. There were notes she needed to write to people before she left.

Going into the library, she sat behind the desk and opened the top drawer looking for pen and paper.

What she found was a legal paper with Katy's name on it.

Christiana sat back in the chair and stared at that drawer. Those were Dillon's private papers. She had no business looking at them without his permission.

But that was Katy's name she'd seen, and Katy was the reason she'd come to Lakecroft in the first place.

Leaning forward, she removed the paper and began to read.

Dillon walked for miles, anger in every step. Angry with himself for trusting Christiana and angry with her for betraying that trust. And angry, perhaps most of all, at a fate that had forced each of them to behave in ways so alien to their basic natures.

He circled the lake and stood staring at the house, but couldn't bring himself to go back in. Not just yet. Instead, he went to the barn and started sanding the rocking chair.

"There you are," Stella said as she walked in, bundled in her coat.

Dillon looked up from what he was doing.

"I heard what happened."

He went back to sanding. "Stay out of this, Stella. It's none of your business."

"You and Katy are my business. You love Christiana and so does that little girl. Don't let her leave here without knowing the truth about her sister."

"I can't tell her about Paige."

"You have to. You're going to lose her if you don't."

"I can't hurt her like that. It's better just to let her go."

"The two of you should listen to yourselves. Look at what she's gone through to help her parents. That girl has probably never told a lie in her life until she came here, and anyone could tell just by looking at her that she's been going through hell. Look at what you've sacrificed to make sure your sister didn't get hurt. Christiana has a right to know the truth about Paige and about your marriage, and you have a duty to tell her. Think about it."

"Stella . . ."

The housekeeper lifted her hand. "That's all I have to say on the matter."

Dillon watched her leave. For a long time he was motionless. Then he threw down his sandpaper and picked up a carving tool.

Christiana found Dillon in the barn. She stood in the doorway, the paper in her hand, and watched him as he worked on the intricate design that fanned the headrest of the rocking chair. The sleeves of his faded blue work shirt were rolled up despite the winter chill in the air.

Dillon knew she was there before he saw her. He stopped working and looked up.

Christiana stepped forward and handed him the paper, her eyes on his face. "I was looking for some writing paper in your desk and happened across this."

Dillon didn't even bother to look at it. He already knew what it was.

"Would you please explain to me why, if Katy is your daughter, you found that it was necessary for you to adopt her after Paige's death?"

He put down his tool. There was no way around it now. "Because," he said with something like resignation in his voice, "she isn't my natural daughter."

Christiana blinked in surprise. "But I thought..."

"You thought from all of the evidence that I'd gotten Paige pregnant and then had to marry her."

"Things seemed to point in that direction."

"I didn't. I didn't sleep with Paige before we got married, and I didn't sleep with her afterward."

"What?" Christina sounded as shocked as she felt.

Dillon shook his head as he looked at her. "Christiana, it won't accomplish anything for me to tell you the whole story. It will only end up hurting a lot of people—especially those parents of yours that you're trying so hard to protect. Let's just say that Paige and I were not a match made in heaven and leave it at that."

She touched his arm. "Dillon, I want to know what happened between the two of you. I need to know. And not just because of Katy."

Dillon looked at her for a long time, finally understanding the truth of her words. He walked away from her and stood with his shoulder against the frame of the open door. Neither of them noticed the cold; so intent were they on the scene playing out between them.

With his back still toward her, he began. "I first met your sister when she used to attend backstage parties after performances of the band. She got to be quite a regular. I never really talked to her because it was my habit to make a short appearance and then leave. Alone."

"She told me about those parties."

"Paige apparently found me to be a challenge. She began showing up at all of our concerts, no matter where we were. And then at the private parties. My sister Anne and her husband Brent, whom you may recall was lead guitarist with the band, threw a birthday party for me. Somehow, Paige found out about it and showed up. It began to seem like every time I turned around, she was there. I couldn't get rid of her, and I couldn't convince her that I wasn't interested. The more I tried, the more obsessed she became.''

Dillon turned and looked at Christiana. ''Sometimes I'm not a very observant person, particularly when my mind's focused on work. I didn't know that Paige and Brent were having an affair. What I did know was that my sister had been diagnosed with terminal cancer.''

He rubbed his forehead. ''You didn't know Anne,'' he said quietly, ''but you would have loved her, Christiana. Everyone did. She was one of the kindest people I've ever known. And she was very much in love with her husband. It would have killed her to know that Brent had been unfaithful—particularly with a woman she'd grown to consider a friend.''

Christiana could see the hurt in his eyes.

''Paige knew about Anne's cancer, and she knew how I felt about my sister. When Paige found herself pregnant with Brent's child, whether by accident or design, she came to me—the one man in the band who wanted nothing to do with her. She had an ultimatum. If I married her, she wouldn't see Brent again, and Anne would never find out that Paige was going to have Brent's child. If I didn't, she'd tell Anne everything.''

Christiana was filled with shame.

''So I married her. And I loathed her every second of every day. And when Katy was born, I didn't care. She wasn't my child. I stayed away as much as

I could. After a while, Paige grew to hate me as much as I hated her. I honestly think that she believed I'd eventually fall in love with her. Then she was killed in the accident. Anne died a few days after that. As far as I was concerned, it was all over. But I'd forgotten about Katy. When I got home, she was still there, in all of her innocence. I thought about putting her up for adoption, but the more I was with her, the more I realized how much she needed me—and how much I'd grown to love her. She couldn't help who her mother was."

"What about her real father?"

"Brent knows Katy's his, but that means nothing to him. He signed away all of his rights to any say in her future. And I adopted her. Katy is legally my daughter now."

Christiana turned away. She couldn't even bear to look at him.

Dillon turned her around, his hands on her shoulders. "I know that wasn't any easier for you to hear than it was for me to say. I'm sorry."

"You're sorry? After what Paige did? After what I did?" She swallowed hard. "No wonder you can't stand my family. I thought I knew my sister pretty well, but I never imagined she'd be capable of something like that." Her eyes met his. "My parents can never know this. It would kill them."

"I'd never tell them."

"Thank you. After what I've done, that's more consideration than I deserve."

"And exactly what is it that you've done, Christiana?"

"Do you mean besides the lying and the sneaking?"

He touched her cheek. "I came out here to think. As it happens, I had a little help from Stella. I put myself into your position."

Her eyes searched his. "And?"

"And no matter how I arrange the facts in my own mind, the conclusion never changes. If I'd been in your situation with the information you had, I would have done the same thing."

"You would?"

"Your motives were good. It was just your execution that was a little awkward. And you were right that I shouldn't judge your parents without even knowing them. They may have raised Paige, but they raised you also, and that's something very much in their favor. I'll have my attorney contact them about visitation. I'd prefer that it take place here until I reach a point where I feel I can trust them with her."

"Thank you, Dillon," she said softly. "That's very generous of you, considering everything that's happened."

He sighed as he cupped her face in his hands and looked into her eyes. "Oh, Christiana, where do we go from here? I meant what I said earlier. I love you."

"I love you, too. I never knew I could love anyone as much as I love you."

"Then stay here with Katy and me. Marry me."

Her throat closed. "I can't."

"You can. All you have to do is say yes."

Her eyes moved over his face feature by feature. "I want to marry you more than anything in the world. I want to be able to love you freely and to watch Katy grow up, but I can't."

"We're back to your parents, aren't we?" he asked, his hands falling to his sides.

"If I marry you without their knowing about what Paige did, they'll feel I've betrayed them and my sister. In their hearts, I'll be as dead as Paige. If I tell them about Paige, it'll be as though I'd killed her twice. I can't be responsible for doing that to them."

"Christiana..."

"And if I did just marry you anyway, how could either of us ever be truly happy knowing what that happiness cost others? I know you understand that, Dillon. I know you understand because now I know what you've sacrificed for your own family."

Dillon had never felt so helpless. The woman he loved was slipping away from him, and there was nothing he could do about it. "Your parents may be stronger than you think."

She looked into his eyes. "Could you destroy your parents' memories of Anne? If you found out something terrible about her, would you tell them, or would you do everything in your power to save them that pain?"

"You know the answer to that."

Christiana walked away from him. She stopped in front of the chair he'd been working on and ran her fingers over the carving. "This is beautiful."

Dillon's eyes narrowed as he watched her. He'd known her for such a short time, and yet he understood her so well. "What is it that you're not telling me?" he asked.

Her fingers stopped moving, then started again. "I'm responsible for Paige's death."

"You're responsible for... What are you talking about?"

"I was the one who was driving the car when we were hit."

Dillon came up behind her and wrapped her in his arms. "Oh, Christiana, don't do this to yourself. A drunk driver is responsible for Paige's death."

"We were talking, Dillon. Maybe if I'd looked instead of just pulling out when the light turned green, I would have seen the other car."

"You do take the guilt of the world and carry it on your shoulders, don't you, Christiana Stevenson?"

"Nothing happened to me. I got out of that car without anything more than scratches and bruises."

"You survived because you were meant to survive. Questioning that won't bring your sister back to life."

She shivered. "I wish I could get the images of that night out of my mind."

Dillon turned her to face him, sudden understanding in his eyes. "You saw the car burn, didn't you?" he asked quietly. "That's what makes you scream in your sleep."

"My sister was in that burning car, and all I could do was watch." Christiana's voice was an agonized whisper.

He pulled her into his arms again. "I'm so sorry. But you can't blame yourself. You must know that.

Nothing that's happened—not with Paige, or me, or your parents—is your fault. Things happen over which we have no control."

"I know that intellectually."

Dillon held her away from him and looked down at her. "Then start to understand it emotionally." He reached out and tucked her hair behind her ears as he looked into her eyes. "You'll never be free of the nightmares until you do."

Christiana's eyes stung with tears. "Oh, I hate this," she said, as she dashed at them with the back of her hand. "I've cried more in the last three months than in my entire life."

"And you're going to cry more. You have a lot of decisions to make."

"Dillon...."

"Let me finish. You and I belong together. We both know that. I think in some strange way we've known that since the moment I almost ran you down with the horse. But I can't make you stay here with me. I wouldn't if I could. You have to come to terms with your parents, with the death of your sister and with what you've learned about her today. But most of all, you have to come to terms with yourself. I want you with me more than I can say, but out of strength, not weakness."

Christiana looked stricken.

"Don't look at me like that," he said gently, as he stroked her damp cheek. "The last thing I want is to hurt you."

"But I'm hurting you."

His eyes moved slowly over her face. "You are not responsible for my happiness. I am. And when you leave here today, I want you to remember that. When you come back to me, do it because it's what you want, not because it's what will make me happy. I won't have you on any other terms."

Dillon picked up his jacket and started to leave. As he got to the door, he paused and turned to her. "It's ironic. Your sister's ability to determine my fate hasn't diminished with her death. She's what brought you into my life in the first place—and she's what's taking you away from me."

Christiana watched him leave. She heard a car door close, then an engine started. She listened until it faded down the road into silence.

There was a rustling noise behind her. "So," came Stella's stern voice from a back door to the barn. "You're leaving."

Christiana jumped and turned around. "How long have you been standing there?"

"Long enough. I can't believe you're really leaving."

"I'm sorry, Stella," Christiana said wearily, "but I can't go through this again. Not today."

"It's going to break Katy's heart when she comes home and you're not here."

"I'm going to Dillon's parents house before I leave the island. I'll explain things to Katy as best I can. But it's not like I'm never going to see her again. And once she gets a new nanny, she'll be fine."

"That's not the same. She loves you."

"I love her, too." Her voice broke on the words.

Stella wrapped Christiana in a big hug. "I learned something a long time ago. The truth can be hard to take. But people survive it. And that's all I have to say on the matter. Now I have work to do."

Left on her own, Christiana stood in the middle of the barn and looked around. The bikes were back on their pegs. Everything was in order. She walked over to the rocking chair and ran her fingers over the wood. Without considering why she did it, Christiana scooped up a handful of woodshavings and put them into her coat pocket. Then she went back to the house.

When she got there, Finn and Ian were lying in front of the fireplace in the library. She knelt down to pet them. "What am I going to do without you if I get caught in another snowstorm?" she asked.

Her eyes went to the telephone. There was one more thing she had to do before she could leave. Walking over to it, she dialed Leslie's number.

"Hello?"

"Hi, John, this is Christiana. Is Leslie there? I need to talk to her."

"I'm afraid not. She won't be back for two, maybe three hours. She took Cameron into town for a little shopping. Want her to call you when she gets in?"

Christiana was almost relieved. Leslie would never have let her get away without explaining everything. "I'm afraid I won't be here then."

"Is everything all right, Chrissie?" John asked. "You sound funny."

"Everything's fine. It's just that I'm leaving Lakecroft, and I wanted to tell her about it myself."

"Leaving Lakecroft? That comes as something of a surprise. What's going on?"

"It's a long story. Let's just say I'm moving on to other things."

"Is there a number where she can reach you? I know she's going to want to talk to you."

"No. I don't even know where I'm going yet. Tell her that I'll call."

"All right. Listen—good luck with whatever you're going to be doing. We're going to miss you."

"I'll miss both of you, too."

As soon as she'd hung up, she carried her things out to her car, then stood in the cold air looking around. Even covered in winter white, she loved this place.

She reached into her pocket and tenderly touched the shavings. "Goodbye, Dillon."

Dillon pulled his car to the side of the road and just sat there. His hands gripped the steering wheel so hard his knuckles were white. Letting her go had been the most difficult thing he'd ever done.

But there was no other way. "Oh, Christiana," he said hoarsely, "come back to me soon."

Chapter Ten

Six months later, Christiana sank into the chair in her hotel room and slit open the large manila envelope containing her forwarded mail. As she separated her personal letters from the bills, she stopped abruptly at one from Leslie. She opened it right away, and some sort of ticket fell out as she unfolded the letter. Christiana glanced at it briefly, then read the letter, her eyes skimming the words, looking for news of Dillon. "I thought you might be interested in this particular performance of The Canadian National Symphony Orchestra, so I'm enclosing a ticket."

Christiana picked up the ticket and looked at it more closely. It read: *The Canadian National Symphony Orchestra with Dillon Austin. Special Performance.* The date was three days away.

She walked to the window and stared down at the street. She'd come to Cairo, Egypt within weeks of leaving Lakecroft, to take the pictures that would grace the pages of a travel book. She'd nearly finished writing the text. There was certainly nothing left to do that she couldn't finish in her own home.

She looked at the ticket again. Her eyes lingered on Dillon's name. There was nothing she wanted more than to hear what Dillon had created. And to see him. Not to talk to him—but just to look at him.

She picked up the phone and called Leslie. "Hi, it's me," she said as soon as she heard Leslie's voice.

"Chrissie! Where are you?"

"Still in Egypt."

"I thought as much. Did you get my letter?"

"The one with the ticket? It came today. That's why I'm calling. Does Dillon know about this?"

"No. I bought the ticket on my own. If—and I know that's a big if—you decide to use it, Dillon won't even be aware that you're there. I knew you'd want it that way."

Christiana sat on the arm of the worn couch. "Thank you, Leslie."

"What do you think you'll do?"

"I don't know."

"It's in three days. You'd better make up your mind."

"I will."

There was a long pause. "He's miserable, Chrissie. I've never seen Dillon like this. He puts on a good front for Katy and his parents, but there are times when I look in his eyes and I see such pain."

Christiana closed her eyes but didn't say anything.

"Won't you tell me what happened between the two of you? Dillon loves you, you love Dillon. Why aren't you together?"

"There are reasons. I wish I could tell you, Leslie, but I can't."

"All right—for now. I'll find out eventually."

"I have to go, Leslie. I'll talk to you soon."

"You take care of yourself."

"I will."

Christiana had no sooner hung up the phone than she realized what her decision was. She was going to the concert.

Lifting the receiver again, she got herself a ticket to Vancouver on the next available flight and started packing.

Christiana timed everything perfectly. She left her luggage at Vancouver International Airport for placement on a connecting flight to Chicago that was leaving in five hours. Then she took a taxi to the Orpheum, an old building set in the very heart of the city.

She showed her ticket to an usher, who handed her a program and directed her to the second level of the theater. The seat was in the front row, just to the left of center stage.

Members of the orchestra were already seated, and they were quietly tuning their instruments or playing a passage to warm themselves up. The result was a low level of pleasant dissonance. A black grand piano was set within a half-moon of the orchestra. There was no conductor's podium.

Christiana leaned back in her seat and gazed around the theater. It was a little like being in the Sistine Chapel with its dome and paintings on the ceiling.

People of all ages filed in continuously until every seat was filled. Then there was an expectant hush. Christiana had just started to look at her program describing the music, and what was behind its creation, when the orchestra grew silent and the lights in the theater dimmed. Dillon stepped out.

Christiana leaned forward as if those few inches would bring her closer to him. He wore a dark suit, white shirt and dark tie with the knot casually loosened.

The audience applauded, but Christiana just watched him as he sat at the piano. She had a perfect view of him. His hair, still long in back, curled over the collar of his shirt.

The theater grew silent. No one even coughed. Dillon looked at the orchestra, raised his hand, then brought it down.

And there was music. Incredible music. Sometimes it was lush and beautiful, sometimes powerful, sometimes full of joy.

Christiana never moved. Her eyes remained unwaveringly on Dillon, watching every move of his body, the expressions on his face. These brief moments would have to last her a lifetime.

At the end, all of the lights on the stage dimmed except the one on Dillon. It was as though he was out there all alone. From the first notes he played next, she recognized the song she'd heard him working on at Lakecroft.

Yet it was different. There was a haunting sadness to it now that caught at her heart. The last notes drifted into silence.

The house lights brightened. For what seemed like ages, no one moved. Then the applause started, slowly at first, then built into a standing ovation. Dillon rose and faced the audience. He didn't seem as happy or as pleased as he should have been.

Even after the orchestra had taken its bow, applause still rocked the theater.

Dillon had been looking out at the audience. Quite suddenly, as though he'd sensed Christiana's presence, he raised his head and looked straight at her. There was a subtle change in his expression.

He stood unmoving, looking at her.

After a minute, people in the audience started turning their heads in her direction.

Neither Christiana nor Dillon noticed, so intent were they on each other.

Christiana's eyes moved over his face, memorizing each feature, cherishing him. In her heart, she said goodbye once again.

Then she turned and left the theater.

It was just before dawn when Christiana got back to her apartment. She set her suitcases in the front hall and flipped on a light. There was a note on the floor that had been slipped under the door. Shrugging off her purse and camera equipment, she sank tiredly onto the couch and opened it. Her mother wanted her to call as soon as she got in.

Christiana looked at her watch. Four o'clock in the morning. That was a little too early. And right now she didn't want to talk to anyone.

She stared blankly at the wall, wondering if she'd ever be happy again.

She couldn't imagine it.

Christiana was asleep on the couch when her intercom beeped. She slowly opened her eyes and lay there, disoriented.

It beeped again.

She made her way to it and leaned tiredly against the wall as she pressed the button. "Who's there?"

"It's me," came her mother's voice. "I need to talk to you."

Christiana pushed the button that unlocked the lobby door and opened her own door to wait. She heard the elevator door open and a moment later, the sound of her mother's light footsteps echoed down the hall.

Marian White hugged her daughter, then stepped back a little and looked at her closely. "You look like hell," she said quietly.

"I just got back—" Christiana looked at her watch "—three hours ago. What are you doing here so early? Where's Dad?"

"He had something he needed to do this morning. He'll meet us here later." Her mother walked into the living room, leaving Christiana to close the door and follow her. For a time, the older woman said nothing, but stood looking out the window with her back to Christiana. Then she suddenly turned, her eyes on her daughter. "Why didn't you tell me what you knew about Paige?"

"What?" Christiana asked helplessly.

"You knew all about how Paige coerced Dillon into marrying her, and evidently you even knew that Dillon isn't Katy's natural father. And yet you never said a word to either your father or myself. I want to know why."

"I didn't think those were things you needed to know."

"You mean that you didn't want to hurt us."

Christiana didn't say anything.

"You should have told us. We had a right to know."

"How did you find out?"

Her mother sat on the couch. "Two months ago, your father and I had our first visitation with Katy. I was, to put it mildly, less than charming to Dillon. That housekeeper of his got upset, and just before we left Lakecroft, she threw every bad thing she knew about Paige into our faces."

"Oh, no." Christiana sank onto the couch next to her mother. "I'm so sorry. What did Dillon say?"

"Dillon wasn't there. He probably still doesn't know what happened. I discounted everything at first, of course, as the rantings of a lunatic who had it out for my beautiful Paige. Your father was rather less surprised than I. But neither of us could let it rest. We finally tracked down this Brent Peters that the housekeeper had mentioned—Katy's natural father—and asked him." Her expression grew unspeakably sad. "He apparently knew Paige quite well, and he confirmed every ugly detail."

"Stella had no right..."

"No, she didn't. But you, on the other hand, had a duty to tell us, C.J., regardless of our emotional fallout. Stella may have had no right to tell us, but we had every right to know. And we should have heard the truth from you."

"I just couldn't do that to you and Dad."

Her mother took Christiana's hand in her own. "You've always had too soft a heart. Ever since you were a little girl. I used to worry about you so much." She looked into Christiana's eyes. "I know I asked you this once before, but I'm going to ask you again. Are you in love with Dillon Austin?"

"Yes."

"And he's in love with you?"

"Yes."

Her mother took a deep breath and slowly exhaled. "I've certainly managed to make a mess of things, haven't I? I got so wrapped up in the death of one daughter that I failed to recognize that I had another who miraculously survived. What I've done to you these past months is inexcusable." She touched Christiana's cheek. "I'm sorry. I know that isn't enough, but I truly am. I want you to go to your Dillon. You should be with him."

Christiana looked at her mother for a moment, her heart in her eyes, then threw her arms around her mother's neck. "Thank you," she whispered.

Her mother hugged her tightly. "I love you so much, C.J. Be happy."

The tiredness that had been etched into Christiana's face had miraculously vanished.

Her mother looked at her watch. "If you leave now, you'll be there by this afternoon."

"I should pack some different clothes..."

"Just take what you have. If you need anything else, you can buy it when you get there. Now go and put poor Dillon out of his misery. My driver is waiting for me downstairs. Tell him I said he should take you straight to the airport. I'll take a taxi home."

Christiana hugged her again.

"That's enough of that. Get going."

Christiana grabbed her purse and camera equipment and her two suitcases and waited impatiently for the elevator. When she finally got downstairs, she nearly ran into her father as he was coming into the lobby. Christiana dropped her luggage long enough to hug him. "I love you, Dad. I know that Mom's change of heart has everything to do with you. Thank you."

He wrapped his arms around his daughter and held her close. "I love you, too, honey. Be happy."

Marian followed her daughter down in the next elevator and stood with her husband as they watched her drive away. He squeezed her hand. "You did the right thing," he said.

"It was a long time coming, though," she said softly.

* * *

It was nearly midnight by the time Christiana got back to Lakecroft. Everything was dark. There wasn't even much of a moon. She knocked on the door and waited.

There was no answer.

She knocked again.

Still there was no answer.

Her hand fell to her side. What if Dillon was still in Vancouver? She hadn't even thought about that.

She heard the dogs barking down by the lake. Within seconds they'd run to her and stood waiting for her to pet them. Christiana fell to her knees and affectionately obliged them, but stopped suddenly. "Wait a minute," she said out loud. "Stella wouldn't close the house up for the night and leave you two out here. Somebody has to be home."

She rose and turned the doorknob. It was unlocked and the door opened.

The dogs followed her in and went straight to the library. Christiana followed them. A fire burned low, in need of a new log. There were no lights on.

"What are you doing here?" Dillon asked.

She looked in the direction of his voice and saw him sitting behind his desk, a drink in his hand. It was too dark for her to see his face.

"I came to see you."

"Like you came to see me last night."

"You weren't supposed to know I was there."

She could feel his eyes on her in the darkness. "I always know when you're in the room with me. And I always know when you leave." He took a drink. "When I saw you last night, for just a moment I thought—I hoped—that you were finally coming back. And then you were gone. I don't think I've ever felt quite so empty."

He got up from the desk and put another log on the fire. For a long time he stood staring into the flames, then he turned to Christiana. "If you've come to see Katy, she's asleep."

"I came to see you."

"Why?"

"Things have changed."

"Changed how?"

She moved closer to him. "My parents know about Paige and what she did."

"Did you tell them?"

"No, I could never have done that no matter how much I wanted to be with you."

"Then how..."

"Stella. She lost her temper with my mother—justifiably so, I'm sure—and told my parents everything."

"Oh, no. I'm so sorry Christiana."

"It hurt them, but they're all right. In fact they're better than all right. I haven't talked to either of them about this as much as I intend to, but Mom seems, in some strange way, better than she was."

His eyes moved over her face. "So what does that mean for us?"

Christiana reached out and touched his beard-roughened cheek. "Dillon, I've grown up a lot during these past months. I've faced some hard truths. I felt guilty about Paige for reasons that went deeper than driving the car she was killed in. There were times when I watched her with my parents, feeling as though I was on the outside looking in, and I wished her gone, the way a child will. And though I got over that as we grew older, I remembered the feeling. And when she really was gone, I felt as though it was my fault. But now I know—and more importantly, I understand—that I didn't do anything wrong. If I could have saved her, I would have."

Dillon covered her hand with his.

"And I also know that it's all right for me to love you. What I feel for you has nothing to do with Paige and everything to do with us. When I was here last time, I always felt as though Paige was between us, like some kind of impenetrable cloud. She's not there any longer. There's just you and me."

"And so you've come back to me," he said quietly.

"If you still want me."

Dillon pulled her into his arms and held her tightly. "If I still want you? I never stopped wanting you. I never will."

Christiana closed her eyes tightly. "You've no idea how afraid I was to come here tonight. I mean, I really wanted to, but I kept trying to imagine what I'd do if you told me to leave and the thought nearly paralyzed me."

Dillon ran his fingers through her silky hair and pushed it away from her face as he looked into her eyes. "I've kicked myself nearly every day since I sent you away the first time. And last night when I saw you, for just a flicker of a moment, I thought you'd come back to me. And in that flicker, I realized how empty everything in my life had grown. Everything but Katy. That night should have been a triumph for me. Instead it became something to get through. Even this place.'' He shook his head. ''Your ghost was everywhere.''

''You were right to send me away before. Everything you said to me that morning was right. I had to come to terms with myself before I could love you the way I was meant to, and before I could accept your love the way I need to. But I've done that now. I'm here and I'm whole.''

Dillon wrapped her in his arms and drew her body close to his. ''I love you.''

As soon as his mouth touched hers, all of the longing Christiana had felt since the day she'd met Dillon welled up and into her kiss. Dillon held her body as close to his as he could, probing her mouth deeply and suggestively.

His hands moved down her sides, over the slender curve of her waist and hip. Christiana could feel how much he wanted her and it made her own passion flame even more.

Dillon stopped suddenly and buried his face in her hair. ''We can't do this.'' His voice was deep and raspy.

''Yes, we can. We love each other.'' She moved her head back and looked into his eyes. ''Dillon, being with you is the most natural thing in the world. It's as though it was always meant to be this way between us.''

He kissed the corners of her mouth. ''I know. I think I've been waiting for you all my life. But when we make love, I want you to be truly mine in every sense of the word. I want to marry you. I want to build a life here, with you.''

"I want that, too."

"Then we'll do things in the right order."

She moved against him. "I don't think I can wait."

Dillon inhaled sharply and kissed her again. "That's not fair."

Her eyes sparkled. "I know."

Dillon sat on the couch and pulled Christiana down with him. He wrapped her in his arms and kissed the top of her head. "I feel so at peace right now. I can't even hate Paige anymore for what she did. Everything fell together to bring you to me."

Christiana grew silent. She was home. For the first time in her life, she was where she truly belonged.

"What are you thinking?" Dillon asked.

She tilted her head and looked up at him. "How lucky I am to be in love and loved by you."

Epilogue

Christiana stood silently staring into the fireplace. Dillon watched her with loving eyes from the doorway for a long time before saying anything.

"What are you thinking, Christiana Austin?" he asked, moving toward her.

She looked up at her husband of just a few hours. "Everything is so perfect that I'm almost afraid to breathe or speak because it might all vanish, like an unfinished dream."

Dillon raised her face to his. "This isn't a dream. You're here, with me, now and forever. Not anything or anyone is ever going to pull us apart again." He lowered his lips to hers and kissed her with a lingering tenderness that filled her with warmth. His strong arms circled around her, drawing her body against his. Christiana tangled her fingers in his hair and held his lips to hers as they both slowly sank to their knees on the rug in front of the fire.

Dillon moved slightly away from Christiana and looked into her eyes as he undid the buttons on the front of her nightgown one by one. With gentle hands, he slid the soft material over her shoulders. It fell in a circle around her hips. His eyes moved slowly over her shapely shoulders and softly rounded breasts, down the curving line of her body to her flat stomach then back up to her eyes. "You're so beautiful," he said softly.

Christiana felt no embarrassment or inhibitions. She wanted to belong to this man as completely as one person could belong to another.

Dillon took her hand in his and held it against his bare chest. She could feel his heart beating in rhythm with her own. Slowly he pulled her body to his until their bare skin touched, then blended together. His hand moved down the curve of her back and held her against him as they kissed. He lowered her gently to the rug and half covered her body with his own.

The kiss grew deeper as each explored every corner of the other's mouth. Dillon's hand moved down the length of her body and up the inside of her silky thigh. She inhaled sharply when his long fingers found their mark and her back involuntarily arched. His mouth moved down over her body to the soft swell of her breast. His tongue teased her erect nipple then his mouth closed over it, making it his. Christiana's fingers tangled in his hair and pressed his mouth more tightly to her as her breath escaped in soft gasps.

Dillon's mouth moved over every inch of her body until he knew it better than she did. Her skin tingled with an awareness that made her tremble with desire.

As Dillon slid his own body up hers, Christiana gently moved him onto his back and began her own exploration down over his solid chest and flat, muscled stomach.

When he could stand it no longer, Dillon groaned and turned Christiana onto her back. He raised himself over her with a hand flat on the floor on either side of her head and looked into her eyes in the flicker of the dying firelight. "I love you."

Christiana pulled his mouth to hers. "I love you, too."

Dillon's elbows bent as his body covered hers. Christiana wrapped her legs around him and pulled him inside her. For a moment, neither of them moved. Dillon looked into her eyes and pushed her hair away from her damp forehead, then he slowly and rhythmically began moving. Their mouths met in a kiss that mimicked what was happening below thrust for thrust. A pressure built up inside them until there was no release for it except the explosion that suddenly rocked them both.

Afterward, Dillon rolled onto his back, pulling Christiana with him, and they lay silently in each other's arms. Dillon rubbed his lips against her hair. "I didn't know it could be like that," he said softly. "I guess I was just going through the motions until tonight."

Christiana raised her head so that she could look into his eyes.

"What are you thinking?" Dillon asked.

"So many things." She touched his face with her hands. "I understand myself now in a way I never did before, because of you. I was so overwhelmed with guilt during the past eight months that I lost my ability to feel anything else. Guilt over arguing with Paige, guilt over her death, guilt over lying to everyone here, but most of all, to you, and guilt over falling so in love with you. There was no way out for me except to spend the rest of my life empty and in pain."

Dillon's eyes moved over her dear face. "You turned yourself into the caretaker of the world, but no one was taking care of you."

"I didn't want anyone to take care of me. Or perhaps I did want it. I just wasn't able to accept it. But I'm free now. Free to love you and to let you love me."

Dillon kissed her tenderly. "Now that I have you, I'm never going to let you go. I made that mistake once."

"It wasn't a mistake. You were right to want me to come to you out of strength, not weakness."

"But at the time, I didn't know if you'd ever return. Christiana, those months without you were the most difficult I've ever lived through. I had to keep up a front for Katy, but that's all it was. Inside, I was empty." He raised her palm to his mouth and kissed it. "You hold my life in your hands. I've never given anyone that much power over me before."

Christiana moved her body closer to his. "Do you think we'll always love each other this much?"

"I can't remember a time when I didn't love you. I can't imagine a time when I won't."

"It's almost frightening." She rested her cheek on his shoulder. "I didn't know I was capable of loving anyone the way that I love you."

Dillon held her close in his strong arms. His hand lightly stroked her hair. "Welcome home, Christiana. Welcome to where you belong."

*   *   *   *   *

**Star-crossed lovers?
Or a match made in heaven?**

Why are some heroes strong and
silent...and others charming
and cheerful? The answer is
WRITTEN IN THE STARS!

Coming each month in 1991,
Silhouette Romance presents
you with a special love story
written by one of your favorite
authors—highlighting the hero's
astrological sign! From January's
sensible Capricorn to December's
disarming Sagittarius, you'll
meet a dozen dazzling and
distinct heroes.

Twelve heavenly heroes...twelve
wonderful Silhouette Romances
destined to delight you. Look for
one WRITTEN IN THE STARS
title every month throughout
1991—only from Silhouette
Romance. STAR

ARE YOU A ROMANCE READER WITH OPINIONS?

Openings are currently available for participation in the 1990-1991 Romance Reader Panel. We are looking for new participants from all regions of the country and from all age ranges.

If selected, you will be polled once a month by mail to comment on new books you have recently purchased, and may occasionally be asked for more in-depth comments. Individual responses will remain confidential and all postage will be prepaid.

Regular purchasers of one favorite series, as well as those who sample a variety of lines each month, are needed, so fill out and return this application today for more detailed information.

1. Please indicate the romance series you purchase from regularly at retail outlets.

Harlequin	Silhouette	
1. ☐ Romance	6. ☐ Romance	10. ☐ Bantam Loveswept
2. ☐ Presents	7. ☐ Special Edition	11. ☐ Other _____
3. ☐ American Romance	8. ☐ Intimate Moments	
4. ☐ Temptation	9. ☐ Desire	
5. ☐ Superromance		

2. Number of romance paperbacks you purchase new in an average month:

    12.1 ☐ 1 to 4   .2 ☐ 5 to 10   .3 ☐ 11 to 15   .4 ☐ 16+

3. Do you currently buy romance   13.1 ☐ yes   .2 ☐ no
   series through direct mail?

If yes, please indicate series: _____
                                                    (14,15)   (16,17)

4. Date of birth: _____ / _____ / _____
                   (Month)   (Day)   (Year)
                    18,19   20,21   22,23

5. Please print:
   Name: _____
   Address: _____
   City: _____ State: _____ Zip: _____
   Telephone No. (optional): (_____) _____

MAIL TO: Attention: Romance Reader Panel
         Consumer Opinion Center
         P.O. Box 1395
         Buffalo, NY 14240-9961   ☐☐☐☐☐☐☐☐☐☐☐☐

                                            Office Use Only   SRDK

Take 4 bestselling love stories FREE

Plus get a FREE surprise gift!

PASSPORT TO ROMANCE
SWEEPSTAKES RULES

1 **HOW TO ENTER:** To enter, you must be the age of majority and complete the official entry form, or print your name, address, telephone number and age on a plain piece of paper and mail to: Passport to Romance, P.O. Box 9056, Buffalo, NY 14269-9056. No mechanically reproduced entries accepted.

2 All entries must be received by the CONTEST CLOSING DATE, DECEMBER 31, 1990 TO BE ELIGIBLE.

3 **THE PRIZES:** There will be ten (10) Grand Prizes awarded, each consisting of a choice of a trip for two people from the following list:
   i) London, England (approximate retail value $5,050 U.S.)
   ii) England, Wales and Scotland (approximate retail value $6,400 U.S.)
   iii) Carribean Cruise (approximate retail value $7,300 U.S.)
   iv) Hawaii (approximate retail value $9,550 U.S.)
   v) Greek Island Cruise in the Mediterranean (approximate retail value $12,250 U.S.)
   vi) France (approximate retail value $7,300 U.S.)

4 Any winner may choose to receive any trip or a cash alternative prize of $5,000.00 U.S. in lieu of the trip.

5 **GENERAL RULES:** Odds of winning depend on number of entries received.

6 A random draw will be made by Nielsen Promotion Services, an independent judging organization, on January 29, 1991, in Buffalo, NY, at 11:30 a.m. from all eligible entries received on or before the Contest Closing Date.

7 Any Canadian entrants who are selected must correctly answer a time-limited, mathematical skill-testing question in order to win.

8 Full contest rules may be obtained by sending a stamped, self-addressed envelope to: "Passport to Romance Rules Request", P.O. Box 9998, Saint John, New Brunswick, Canada E2L 4N4.

9 Quebec residents may submit any litigation respecting the conduct and awarding of a prize in this contest to the Régie des loteries et courses du Québec.

10 Payment of taxes other than air and hotel taxes is the sole responsibility of the winner.

11 Void where prohibited by law

COUPON BOOKLET OFFER TERMS

To receive your Free travel-savings coupon booklets, complete the mail-in Offer Certificate on the preceeding page, including the necessary number of proofs-of-purchase, and mail to: Passport to Romance, P.O. Box 9057, Buffalo, NY 14269-9057 The coupon booklets include savings on travel-related products such as car rentals, hotels, cruises, flowers and restaurants. Some restrictions apply. The offer is available in the United States and Canada. Requests must be postmarked by January 25, 1991 Only proofs-of-purchase from specially marked "Passport to Romance" Harlequin® or Silhouette® books will be accepted. The offer certificate must accompany your request and may not be reproduced in any manner. Offer void where prohibited or restricted by law. LIMIT FOUR COUPON BOOKLETS PER NAME, FAMILY, GROUP, ORGANIZATION OR ADDRESS. Please allow up to 8 weeks after receipt of order for shipment. Enter quickly as quantities are limited. Unfulfilled mail-in offer requests will receive free Harlequin® or Silhouette® books (not previously available in retail stores), in quantities equal to the number of proofs-of-purchase required for Levels One to Four, as applicable.

PR-SWPS

OFFICIAL SWEEPSTAKES
ENTRY FORM

Complete and return this Entry Form immediately—the more Entry Forms you submit, the better your chances of winning!
- Entry Forms must be received by **December 31, 1990**
- A random draw will take place on **January 29, 1991**
- Trip must be taken by **December 31, 1991**

3-SR-3-SW

YES, I want to win a PASSPORT TO ROMANCE vacation for two! I understand the prize includes round-trip air fare, accommodation and a daily spending allowance.

Name_____

Address_____

City_____ State_____ Zip_____

Telephone Number_____ Age_____

Return entries to: **PASSPORT TO ROMANCE**, P.O. Box 9056, Buffalo, NY 14269-9056

COUPON BOOKLET/OFFER CERTIFICATE

Item	LEVEL ONE Booklet 1	LEVEL TWO Booklet 1 & 2	LEVEL THREE Booklet 1, 2 & 3	LEVEL FOUR Booklet 1, 2, 3 & 4
Booklet 1 = $100+	$100+	$100+	$100+	$100+
Booklet 2 = $200+		$200+	$200+	$200+
Booklet 3 = $300+			$300+	$300+
Booklet 4 = $400+				$400+
Approximate Total Value of Savings	$100+	$300+	$600+	$1,000+
# of Proofs of Purchase Required	4	6	12	18
Check One	____	____	____	____

Name_____

Address_____

City_____ State_____ Zip_____

Return Offer Certificates to: **PASSPORT TO ROMANCE**, P.O. Box 9057, Buffalo, NY 14269-9057

Requests must be postmarked by **January 25, 1991**

- ✂ - - - -

ONE PROOF OF PURCHASE

3-SR-3

To collect your free coupon booklet you must include the necessary number of proofs-of-purchase with a properly completed Offer Certificate

See previous page for details